Praise for
The Kingdom Series

"This is one of the best series I have ever read! These books are so gripping and rich in biblical truths that I just couldn't get enough and started reading them over again today!"
—SABRINA

"Ever since John Bunyan's *The Pilgrim's Progress,* few attempts to put biblical truth into allegorical form in stories have been successful or worthily written. The new Kingdom Series is a delightful exception that we are thankful to recommend."
—DENNIS, Grace & Truth Books

"The Kingdom Series contains some of the best books I have ever read! They can stand beside the best like Lewis's *Chronicles of Narnia* and Tolkien's *Lord of the Rings.* Thanks for such great books with a legit message!"
—COLE, age 14

"An amazing book! It puts Christianity in a true perspective."
—DYLAN, age 13

"The story line, characters, and vivid descriptions are fantastic. And, above all, I love how this series parallels the Bible."
—CAROL JO

Look for other books in the Kingdom Series:

Kingdom's Dawn (Book One)
Kingdom's Hope (Book Two)
Kingdom's Edge (Book Three)
Kingdom's Call (Book Four)
Kingdom's Quest (Book Five)

THE KINGDOM SERIES

BOOK 6

KINGDOM'S REIGN

CHUCK BLACK

MULTNOMAH

KINGDOM'S REIGN

Scripture quotations and paraphrases are taken from the New King
James Version®. Copyright © 1982 by Thomas Nelson Inc. Used by permission.
All rights reserved.

The characters and events in this book are fictional, and any resemblance to
actual persons or events is coincidental.

Trade Paperback ISBN 978-1-59052-682-8
eBook ISBN 978-0-307-56185-5

"Reign of the King" music and lyrics copyright © 2006 by Emily Elizabeth Black

Illustrations by Marcella Johnson, copyright © 2006 Perfect Praise Publishing

Published in association with The Steve Laube Agency, LLC, 5501 North
Seventh Avenue, #502, Phoenix, AZ 85013

Published in the United States by Multnomah, an imprint of the Crown
Publishing Group, a division of Penguin Random House LLC, New York.

MULTNOMAH® and its mountain colophon are registered trademarks of Penguin
Random House LLC.

Library of Congress Cataloging-in-Publication Data
Black, Chuck.
    Kingdom's reign / Chuck Black. — 1st ed.
        p. cm. — (The kingdom series ; bk 6)
    ISBN 978-1-59052-682-8
    I. Title.
PS3602.L264K575 2007
813'.6—dc22
                                                    2007000507

Printed in the United States of America
2020

20 19 18 17 16 15

To the King and His Son!

CONTENTS

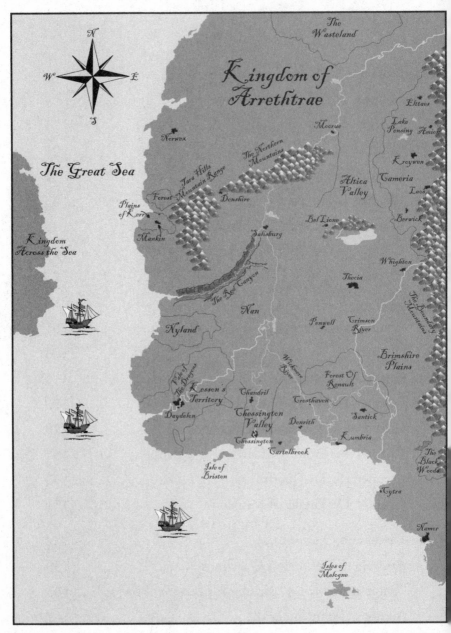

© Chuck Black

EVIL'S BATTLE

Before me lies the grand city of Chessington. I have been away for a number of years, and I do not return to a city of joy, but to one of great apprehension. You see, I am one of thousands here, all ready for battle…the battle of the ages.

My name is Cedric. Through the tales of gallant knights such as Sir Leinad and Sir Gavinaugh, and through the tales of my own life, I have shared with you the story of the people of Arrethtrae, our kingdom. Few are as fortunate as you and I, for most have not let the history of our land or the promise of our future penetrate their hearts with true understanding. It is not by any measure of witty writing that my story will move your heart, but by the sheer truth of the mercy of a King and the sacrifice of His Son. It will change you for its hearing.

Leinad saw the birth of our kingdom and the promise of a deliverer. Unfortunately, he also saw the waning of belief in this hope. I, Cedric of Chessington, saw the fulfillment of the promise Leinad awaited. It came from across the Great Sea in the form of a man—not just any man, but the Prince Himself. He came dressed in the rags of a peasant and taught of His Father the King. Many believed Him, but most did not. I saw the fire in His eyes, the mercy in His acts, the love in His heart, and the power in His words. He trained me and the other Knights of the Prince in the art of the sword. The Prince was a master swordsman, and we became an extension of His mighty arm. He taught that without belief in the Code, the sword was meaningless and even detrimental to the kingdom, for it was the Code that brought allegiance to the King and compassion for our fellow man.

My time with the Prince was precious, albeit short-lived. Those in power considered Him a threat—a threat to be silenced—and so they killed Him. The Prince died for me, for you…for us all. My grief was deep and my sorrow without measure. But then, through the majestic power of the King, the Prince arose and lives again! Yes, He lives again! I must say it twice, lest I question the believability of my own memory, for that day shook the very foundation of the kingdom and will bring its enemy, the Dark Knight, to his knees once and for all.

The Prince left us and returned to His Father across the Great Sea. We did not want Him to go, but it was His way. He came to prepare us for our mission in the kingdom, which was to tell others about Him and train them for the ultimate battle to come. Those years He was away seemed long and without end, but every day we rose to fill the kingdom with the good news of the Prince and His love for the people of Arrethtrae. His life and His teachings possess the power to change the very hearts of men—even mighty men such as Sir Gavinaugh, who was at one time a fierce enemy of the Prince and His Followers.

During these waiting years, we traveled to the far reaches of the kingdom, endured many hardships, and saw strange happenings of all sorts, but those tales are for another day. Eventually the Prince came back for us...for all the Knights of the Prince and for those who were loyal to Him. He took us across the Great Sea to be with Him and the King. It was a reprieve from the persecution that was mounting in the end days, but it was not the end of our mission as His knights—it was the beginning of a new mission!

It is on that voyage home, to the Kingdom Across the Sea, that my story resumes. Upon my steed, as we await the massive evil force that comes to destroy our beloved city, there is a final moment to reflect back on my away years...years that bring understanding to this impending battle.

I remember the night that Keef, a mighty Silent Warrior, awakened me from a deep sleep to board the ships that would take us home. The Prince came to gather His people and take us across the Great Sea to be with the King.

My encounter with the Prince was by far the most life-changing event I have ever experienced. Seeing Him alive again after witnessing His death was the most kingdom-shaking event I have ever experienced. But perhaps the *strangest* moment in my life was when I encountered an old friend...

CHAPTER ONE

THE JOURNEY HOME

 I left the Prince's embrace to board one of the many ships that waited to take us across the Great Sea. For a time, my mission in Arrethtrae was complete. I had yearned to reunite with the One who gave me purpose in life. I had worked to serve Him with honor and faithfulness while He was away. And He gave me the words I craved: "Well done, Cedric. Well done." Like a man arriving home after a long journey, I found rest in His words and in His embrace.

The Prince first came to Arrethtrae to save the kingdom and change the hearts of the people. There is no other like Him…no other who is worthy of the loyal service of all. The Son of the King came as a peasant and served us before we could serve Him. His nature is pure and His heart compassionate. His words are wise and His vision sure. I will follow Him to death, if need be. But I know in my heart of hearts that He will lead us only to life. The road has not and will not be easy, but I will follow, for He is great and His plans are grand.

The ships we boarded were gallant, three-masted vessels with a full rigging of sails that beckoned the wind from a dozen seas to carry them into their waters. They were sturdy yet built for speed. The main deck of each ship was over thirty paces from stem to stern with a quarterdeck and a half-deck above. A lower deck provided space for supplies and for most of the passengers. All of the ships' crews were comprised of Silent Warriors who were very experienced seamen. Conversation with the crew was limited, for they assumed their duties onboard with the utmost diligence.

On the main deck of my ship, I searched the faces of my many companions. I looked for William, my lifelong friend, but I discovered that he had boarded another ship, as had Rob and Barrett. Commanded to be silent, for the entire kingdom was asleep and the exodus of the Knights of the Prince and His people was not complete, I smiled and nodded my greetings to my fellow workers who sat upon the deck. We were going home! It sounded strange yet felt perfect, for this home was a place we had never been, but the King awaited us there. *What will this great kingdom be like?* I wondered.

Our ship launched out into the sea, and I found a place of solitude near the bow, beneath the foresail. The wind in my face and the sound of the waves breaking on the bow took me back to a time when I was a fisherman, before I ever knew of the Prince. As Arrethtrae faded into the horizon, I found myself lost in thoughts of wonderment at the path my life had taken. Long after the coasts of Arrethtrae had disappeared, my solitude was interrupted by a solid voice behind me.

"Sir, I'm sorry to disturb you," the young man said somewhat hesitantly, "but I feel I must introduce myself."

I looked up into the bright face of a handsome young man and rose to my feet. "You are not disturbing me at all," I said with a smile as I offered my hand. "I am Cedric of Chessington."

"I know who you are, sir," he said enthusiastically as he took my hand. "For many years I have desired to meet you again."

"Then we have met before?"

"Yes…when I was but a youth. I am Cullen of the United Cities of Cameria."

I felt such joy to know that the words of the Prince had brought people from the distant lands of Cameria to these ships this day. I recognized his accent from that region. It was unique in that it seemed to mesh the accents of all lands into one.

I released Cullen's hand. "Unto this day, the people of Chessington are indebted to the great land of Cameria and her people," I said. "These final days in Chessington were only bearable in large part because of your people and your help against her enemies."

My words to him were not flattery. Cameria was one of the last regions in the kingdom to hear the story of the Prince, and I had made one of the first journeys there. They embraced the truth of the Prince with eager hearts and quickly became a beacon of light for the entire kingdom. When much of the kingdom turned against Chessington, the five United Cities of

Cameria stood firm in their support of the King's city and His people. Supplies of food and swords were sent without request for trade. But in the final days, even Cameria began to waver as the return of the Prince seemed to linger.

Cullen smiled at the compliment I offered and momentarily looked down in respectful humility. When he lifted his eyes to mine again, I saw the spark of life in him that only a believer had.

"Sir Cedric," he said. "I heard your words of the Prince that day many years ago, and my heart nearly burst within my chest!"

His eyes gleamed, and his countenance radiated with enthusiasm. I could imagine the excitement with which he had shared the story of the Prince with others.

Cullen stood tall and confident. His build was average, but his cheekbones and chin were sharp. His hair was a common brown, but his dark eyes were not common at all.

He continued. "I wanted to believe your words with all of my heart, but it seemed too good to be true. I gave every ounce of my being to live by the Code and learn the ways of the Prince. I guess I needed to prove that it would change my circumstances. It worked, but I was not prepared for the biggest change of all—in myself! I found purpose for my life and a cause much greater than any selfish venture I thought I desired." He smiled broadly. "Thank you, Sir Cedric…thank you!"

I placed my hand on his shoulder. "Cullen, your words have made all of my journeys worth every step. You do not need to thank me, for as you discovered, I cannot contain the hope that was given to me."

In the midst of the Great Sea, our homecoming was already beginning.

"Have you any family onboard, Cullen?"

"Yes…some," he said with a mix of emotions.

I felt a bit foolish for asking the question, since the story of the Prince often split family members' loyalties. Our voyage across the sea this day clarified the permanence that such a separation of hearts within a home caused.

Cullen spoke again. "My parents and my next younger sister would not accept the truth of the Prince and His promise."

"I'm sorry."

A smile crossed his lips. "But glory to the King, my little sister, Keely, is here with me." It was clearly a comfort to him.

"Excuse me, gentlemen, does this young lady belong to either of you?" The question came from a young woman, who was as pretty as her voice. She was guiding a girl toward us who looked as though she'd been caught with her hand in the cookie jar.

Cullen's smile disappeared as he looked down at the lass. "What have you been up to, Keely?"

I could tell in an instant that the girl was as spunky as a tree squirrel. She couldn't contain the broad grin that spread across her freckled face. It was a look of curiosity more than mischief that lit up her eyes.

"I just wanted to see," she said as she pointed up to the crow's-nest at the top of the mainmast.

"I'm sure she would have made it if I hadn't stopped her halfway up," replied her chaperon, a grin on her face as well.

Keely turned to the young lady. "I'm sorry, miss. I'll not try it again."

I found it difficult not to gaze at the woman who had brought Cullen's little sister to him. I wondered what kind of lady would climb the rope ladder to the crow's-nest to apprehend a curious girl when any number of Silent Warrior crewmen could have taken care of the matter. She seemed to have authority of some sort onboard the ship. Her attire was not of the style one might see most Arrethtraen ladies wear. Her blouse and trousers were loose fitting, but were tight at the waist, ankles, and wrists. A three-quarter cape fell from her shoulders to her thighs. It was not the apparel of any I'd ever seen, but it suited her well. Her hair was long, dark brown, and tied in a single braid that fell midway down her back. Yet it was the beautiful sword hanging at her waist that truly set her apart from most other women.

She placed a friendly hand on Keely's head. "See to it, little miss," she said firmly but kindly, "or the captain will have a word with you. And you won't find him nearly as forgiving."

"I'm sorry," said Cullen, slightly embarrassed. "I'll keep a closer eye on her." He looked sternly at Keely, but she didn't seem bothered by it a bit.

I bent down to Keely. "Hello, Keely. I am Cedric."

She confidently held out her hand. "I'm pleased to meet you, Sir Cedric. Cul says you're the best swordsman in the kingdom!"

I shook her hand. "I can hold my own, Keely, but there are many men...and women"—I added as an afterthought and stole a quick glance at the young lady standing behind the girl—"that are as skilled with the sword as I."

"You mean like Talea?" she asked.

"And who is Talea?"

Keely pointed to the woman behind her.

"Pleased to meet you, gentlemen." Talea bowed her head slightly. I was thankful she didn't offer her hand since I wouldn't have known whether to kiss it or shake it.

"I am Cedric of Chessington," I said with a bow, "and this is Cullen of the United Cities of Cameria."

Talea's businesslike countenance did not dim her brown eyes, which sparkled with life. I imagined that a younger Talea wrestled with the same spunky spirit Keely seemed to possess. Although the morning sun had not yet broken the horizon, I could see a noble look upon her face that was woven into every feature from her brow to her chin. She looked into my eyes without hesitation, and I was somewhat mesmerized, for I seemed to gain energy from her gaze. It was not a look of affection but one of question and resolve. Then, for one brief instant, a nearly imperceptible look of embarrassment crossed her face.

"Which region of Arrethtrae are you from?" I asked.

Talea seemed to struggle to find an answer to my question and then reached for her sword. Her face became tense, and her eyes seemed to gaze clean through me and into the receding darkness beyond. The lighthearted mood of our conversation quickly transformed into a moment of uncertain stress. I could tell by Talea's expression that something was wrong, and I naturally moved my hand closer to my sword. In an instant, the building anxiety exploded.

Talea drew her sword and yelled, *"Get dow—!"*

The last of her warning was cut off by the most hideous screech I have ever heard. It was of such a nature that our first reaction was to drop to the deck for cover. Talea brought a powerful upward slice to bear on a winged creature that screamed past our heads from behind. She followed the slice by dropping to the deck herself, but her blade had found its mark. The screech of the attacking beast became the momentary wail of a mortally wounded monster. It hit the side rail of the ship with a solid thud and careened over the edge to the frothy waters below. The entire encounter happened so quickly that I scarcely got a glimpse at the creature. Its body and wings looked dark and leathery, but that was all I could see in the receding darkness of the early morning dawn.

Talea was immediately to her feet, shouting a warning to all passengers to get below deck. One of the larger crewmen came toward us with his sword drawn and a concerned look on his face.

"Are you hurt, Lady Talea?" he asked.

"No, Yutan, I am unharmed," she said. The large warrior seemed satisfied and hurried off. The captain ordered a trumpet blast to warn the other ships, and it spread through the armada rapidly. Cullen grabbed Keely and took her below, while I helped Talea and the crew get the remaining passengers to safety, closing the hatch behind us. I could hear an occasional screech in the distance but nothing quite as close as our first encounter.

The captain and another Silent Warrior remained on deck to ensure that we stayed on course. Everyone else was ordered to remain below for a time. I found a place to sit near the hatch, and Talea sat a few feet away, facing me.

"What in the kingdom was that?" I asked.

She paused. "It was a scynth."

I thought for a moment. "I have never heard of nor seen such a thing. Where do they come from?"

Talea looked at the floor. "They come from the caverns on the Isle of Sedah. Their presence can mean only one thing: all of the evil power of Lucius has been unleashed upon Arrethtrae."

The last few years in Arrethtrae had been tremendously difficult for the Knights of the Prince, but Talea seemed to indicate that it was only the beginning.

"The years ahead will be the darkest the kingdom has ever seen." Talea looked up at me. "We can be grateful to the King and the Prince that we are not there."

Bewildered, I looked at Talea. I did not like a mystery, and she most certainly was one. "Who are you, my lady?"

"I am Talea. Who are you, sir?" she replied tersely.

"I am sorry for the frankness of my question, my lady," I said. "But your skill, your understanding, and your attire are uncommon."

"Is that an insult or an observation, sir?"

"Above all, my lady, it is not an insult. It is an observation and a compliment to one who has stirred my curiosity, dare I say, beyond the bounds of appropriate questioning. Please forgive me."

Talea raised an eyebrow and overwhelmed me once again with her delightful eyes. I felt my cheeks flush, and I wanted to leave…but also wanted to stay. Were it not for the mystery of her presence, I would have departed to spare myself the strangeness I felt within.

"What do you want to know, Sir Cedric?" Talea asked.

I peered into her face. "It would be selfish and unfair of me not to offer answers to your questions first…if you have any."

"I have none," she replied matter-of-factly.

I was oddly offended, since either I was not worthy of her asking or she knew much more about me than I imagined. I chose to believe the latter.

"Very well, Lady Talea. Which region of Arrethtrae are you from?"

"I am not," she said, rather seeming to enjoy the fullness of my perplexed look.

"You are not?"

She smiled. "I am not from any region in Arrethtrae."

"Then you are from many regions?"

She thought for a moment. "I am not."

I found myself quickly becoming frustrated with this pretty and uncommon lady. I was not used to being played. With any other lady, I might think she was flirting, but there was enough mystery and genuine hesitation in Talea's willingness to give answers that I knew this was not the case.

"Then you cannot be from Arrethtrae," I said, trying to reason this through. "But all men and women are from Arrethtrae." A strange thought entered my mind. "Are you a"—I almost could not say it—"Silent Warrior?" If she were a Silent Warrior, she was unique indeed.

She gazed into my bewildered eyes. "I am not."

"Lady Talea, you say you are not from Arrethtrae. You say you are not a Silent Warrior. You know things of which I have not heard. You are obviously very skilled with the use of a sword. I am afraid you are more of a mystery to me now than before!" I said.

"All clear!" came a shout from the main deck.

Talea began to rise. I quickly stood and offered my hand to help her, but she pretended not to see it.

"Will you tell me who you are, Lady Talea?" I asked.

She positioned her sword and straightened her cape. "Perhaps," she said with a slight smile and moved past me to the hatch that led to the main deck.

I had never felt quite so disregarded in all my life. I often found it uncomfortable to be in the presence of a lady when polite conversation was required, but this was different. Talea was more warrior than lady, and yet she moved between both roles so gracefully that I found myself in a social quandary. I intended to avoid much future interaction, simply to prevent the feelings of awkwardness that come with an inadequate repertoire of social graces.

I almost believed it possible to do so, but a corner of my mind would not rest with the mystery of Talea so brazenly unsolved.

CHAPTER TWO

THE
WELCOME

 The remainder of the voyage was largely uneventful. The scynths did not return, and I learned that our encounter with them was unusual. Most of the Silent Warriors, in fact, had never seen them before.

Cullen and I became instant friends and enjoyed many long hours of discourse. Conversation was easy, and he was refreshing to talk to. I learned much more about Cameria and hoped to one day spend time there. Keely was a spry lass who filled the air with exuberance wherever she went. She coerced me into giving her a few fencing lessons and was a quick study.

As for Talea, she was preoccupied with ship duties for most of the voyage, and our encounters had indeed been limited and casual at best. The journey ended with as much mystery about her as when it began.

After many days at sea, the armada of gallant ships finally

arrived at the coasts of the Kingdom Across the Sea. The land looked truly magnificent.

At the docks, the ships cycled through to unload their precious cargo from Arrethtrae: loyal Followers of the King and the Prince. It was a lengthy process, for there were many. We disembarked, and I thanked the crew of Silent Warriors for their labor. I bowed to Talea and bid her farewell. She responded politely in like manner, and I supposed I would not see her again or ever know who she truly was. I was disappointed but did not wish to look the fool and press the matter when it was not my place to do so.

We boarded charming carriages that followed a roadway for some distance. Cullen, Keely, and I managed to share the same carriage with five others. The caravan of carriages stretched on as far as the eye could see both fore and aft of our own. I could only assume that the Prince Himself was at the head of our procession.

The scenery was breathtaking. Tall green trees and lush grass covered the valleys and hills. The wildflowers were fragrant and beautiful. Mingled within the fragrance of the flowers was a familiar but distant sweet odor that took me back to my first encounter with the Silent Warriors when I first met my dear friend Keef. There was a much stronger scent to the healing salve that was applied to William's wound than what I smelled here, but it was the same, I was certain—pleasant and

unusual. One particular wildflower I had never seen before was more prevalent than all the others. I did not know its name, but its greenery grew low to the ground like clover, and the small green leaves gave way every so often to a tender rose-colored flower.

I was taken with the beauty of a landscape that seemed only possible in the mind of a skilled artist. I felt as though I could reach out and touch the canvas upon which it was painted, but I could not, for it was as real as the delicious air I was breathing. The carriage gently swayed back and forth. My fellow companions were as taken with the country as I, and very little conversation ensued.

We traveled through a break in the mountainous terrain and entered the sanctuary of the kingdom. What opened before us was more magnificent than anything I had ever seen. The King's grand city gleamed in the sunlight and sat cradled in the arms of majestic snow-peaked mountains to the north. The lower portion of the city was bordered by a crystal-blue sea. The city spread across the lush, hilly countryside of the foothills and meshed with a rugged granite base that framed the city's edge nearest the sea to the south. A sparkling river flowed from the mountains through the city. On the side nearest our approach, the river exited the city and spilled over granite cliffs into the sea below. Mist rose from the frothy waters of the waterfall to blanket the granite base upon which the city was built. Toward the western edge, granite outcroppings isolated the turbulent waters of the fall from the rest of the sea. The waters became so calm and clear beyond that it looked like crystal-blue glass.

I could not absorb the beauty that surrounded me, and I fear my words are wholly inadequate to describe it.

As we approached, I slowly became aware of how vast the city truly was. I had heard from Leinad that Daydelon, in its days of glory, was a wonder to behold, but I'm sure this City of the King must be one thousand times beyond that ancient city both in size and beauty. I could hardly make myself grasp its existence.

The spires of many palaces rose to the sky from the city's landscape. In the midst of this grand city rose the majestic towers of the King's palace.

The caravan skirted the sea to the left a short distance and then entered the city across a large granite bridge that arched over the waters below. Beyond the bridge was an enormous courtyard that lay before the city gate. Here we left our carriage and joined the growing host of loyal Followers who were gathering at the gate of the city. Fifty massive Silent Warriors stood guard at the gate that offered entrance to the city. They wore full battle dress, with gold trim on their armor. Each held a sword in one hand and a golden trumpet in the other. They stood silent and still…waiting.

As the carriages continued to arrive, we found friends to talk to and shared our wonderment.

"Cedric! Cedric!"

I heard my name called and turned to see my lifelong friend William.

"William!" I exclaimed and ran to meet him.

We embraced with the love of brotherhood. It had been

many days since I'd seen him, and I was delighted to hear his voice and see him again.

"William! It is good to see you!"

"And you, my brother!" he replied. "Isn't this amazing?" he said, sweeping his arm across the glorious scene.

"Indeed, my friend," I said with a silly grin on my face. "Did you ever dream of such a place as this?"

He laughed and shook his head.

"Have you seen Rob or Barrett?" I asked.

"Yes, we traveled on the same ship together. I left them just there," he said, pointing to a group of people.

We approached, and I was once again reunited with my friends and fellow warriors of many years. I introduced Cullen to William, Rob, and Barrett. Rob's smile was as big as ever I'd seen, and Barrett was more peaceful than the crystal sea beyond the city. Something unusual was taking place, and I didn't know what it was. Each of my friends seemed somehow greater than I'd remembered. I attributed it to the majestic surroundings and the excitement of the moment, but even I felt quite different. I took a deep breath and was all the more invigorated.

"What now, my dear fellow companions?" I asked.

"We wait, I guess, for the rest of the carriages," replied Barrett.

As the passengers of one carriage disembarked, I saw Keanna step out and behold the beauty around her. I went to greet her and could see a look of great expectation in her eyes. Her journeys with Sir Gavinaugh throughout the kingdom of Arrethtrae as a Knight of the Prince had won her a place of honor among the legends of great knights, especially when she carried on the great mission of the King after Gavinaugh fell in battle and was taken across the sea.

"Welcome home, Keanna." I bowed to her.

Her face seemed to glow as she looked to the grand city beyond the gates. "Cedric...I never imagined it could be so beautiful!"

"Yes...and we are yet on the outside. I think perhaps the wonders within will overwhelm us."

She broke her gaze from the splendor of the scene and looked at me. Her eyes sparkled. "Do you think I will see him?"

"I do."

She looked back at the city, and I wondered if she was going to burst from the anticipation of her reunion with Gavinaugh.

"Come. Please join us," I said and led her to our group of friends.

The last of the carriages finally arrived, and the massive courtyard was filled with thousands of people. Shortly thereafter, all the Silent Warriors came to a position of readiness, raised their trumpets, and sounded three brilliant notes in unison. One noble Silent Warrior stepped forward and stood before the people. Our congregation became intently silent to listen for whatever message was to come.

"I am Micalem—keeper of the City of the King. Who is worthy to enter?" He asked the question with great authority.

A second Silent Warrior came forward to stand beside him. "What deems a man worthy?" he asked for all to hear.

Micalem responded with a shout. "He is worthy who has

followed the Code without fault. He is worthy who has honored the King with his life and sworn allegiance to Him and Him only. He is worthy who has served the King in truth, justice, and honor. He is worthy who has offered compassion to the weak, the destitute, the widowed, and the poor. He is worthy who has lived for the King and served others without personal gain. He is worthy who has never abandoned a fellow knight in battle or in peril. He is worthy who has equipped, trained, and prepared for battle against the forces of the Dark Knight. He is worthy who has served the King and fainted not in the day of battle. He is worthy who has not used the sword to seek selfish gain but executed justice and the will of the King. He is worthy who has been merciful, loyal, courageous, faithful, and noble, but above all, who has been humble before the King and before men. He is worthy whose words have always been spoken in truth."

He paused and looked over the people in the courtyard. No one uttered a sound.

"Who here has fulfilled every article of the Code and is worthy to enter the gate of the City of the King?" he asked again.

No one dared move, for we all had failed in some way and were not worthy. It was a solemn moment broken only by a stirring at the back of the courtyard furthest from the gate. Soon all eyes turned to behold what manner of man would dare come forward to meet such a challenge. The throng of people parted to give way for the man's approach to the gate. As the man passed by, people began to kneel, until He was before all and all were kneeling. He stood before the massive

Silent Warrior, who suddenly did not look quite as noble with this man near him.

Micalem opened his hands and spread them low before the Prince. "Only You are worthy, my Prince!" he exclaimed and knelt down before Him.

The remaining Silent Warriors also knelt before the Prince and exclaimed in unison, "Only He is worthy!"

The Prince, dressed in royal robes, turned to face us and lifted His hands into the air as if to enclose us in His embrace. "These are worthy, for I died for them and they believed in Me! Open the gates, and welcome them home!"

The Silent Warriors stood, opened the gates, and blasted forth a song of triumph on their golden trumpets. The people all stood and cheered, for our joy was full and our hearts were home. We were delivered and redeemed, and the Prince had brought us home!

CHAPTER THREE

AN "OLD" FRIEND

 Once within the walls of the city, we were greeted with pomp and ceremony. It was a time of great celebration. I saw the gallant Sir Gavinaugh waiting to embrace Keanna, and she ran to him. Their reunion brought tears of joy to us all, for we knew the longing in her heart when he was taken from her. He looked strong and whole once again.

The Prince had prepared a home for each of us that was every bit a palace. We rested for one day, and the following evening we anticipated a grand feast with the King. The beauty of the King's palace was indescribable. Gold, jewels, elegant tapestries, polished marble floors, archways, balconies, towers, fountains, and lush gardens proclaimed magnificence throughout. The inner courtyard was set to accommodate the thousands of new residents at a feast beyond imagination. The head table was set on the marble deck, and the Prince sat to the King's right.

The majesty of the King seemed to radiate in all directions. A jeweled crown sat upon His brow, and a royal robe flowed around Him. As He gazed across the court of loyal knights, His countenance strengthened the hearts of all. The Prince had His Father's eyes, and they too burned like fire. But today the fire was warm, and His joy was obvious to all who saw Him. His people were here to celebrate their homecoming, and He was pleased!

The supper was splendid. Every dish was palate perfection…and there were many.

After the feast, there was music and fellowship. I became reacquainted with many friends I had not seen in years. Once I released the burden of apprehension I had continually fought in Arrethtrae, it was a joyous time. In spite of this, something strange nagged at me, but I could not put my finger on it.

Of all my reunions, one was foremost in my mind. I searched the mass of celebratory people hoping to find an old friend—Leinad. I consciously pushed away the possibility that he might have died—he had been an old man when he was taken from Arrethtrae so many years before. I began asking people about him, but no one knew where he was. My search was reminiscent of the last time I had tried to find him in Arrethtrae. That search, however, had ended sadly, and my heart began to ache. As I continued looking, I found William once again.

"William, do you think it possible that our old friend Leinad might still live?" I asked.

William looked sad. "I have searched and searched, Cedric, but to no avail. Surely the Prince will know. Perhaps we can inquire of Him."

"Gentlemen, can I help you with something?" The question came from behind us.

We turned to see a handsome and refined gentleman who looked to be a few years older than I.

"If only you could, sir," I said. "But I am afraid we are looking for someone that only the Prince would know of."

"What does he look like?" the man asked politely. "Maybe I can help you find him."

The thought seemed futile since even William and I, who knew what Leinad looked like, could not find him. I had no desire to describe Leinad's appearance to the man, so I waited for William to respond, but he did not. I looked his way, and William seemed bewildered and lost in thought.

I turned back to the gentleman. "He is an older man, and I'm afraid his health may have failed him by now. I fear he has passed on, though I cannot be sure."

I glanced at William to see if he had returned from wherever his mind had taken him. He no longer looked bewildered; he looked downright afraid.

"Ah, Cedric and William," the man said.

I turned back to the man, and the hairs on the back of my neck began to tingle. Something bizarre was awakening in my mind. William grabbed my arm and stepped back, pulling me with him. His eyes were fixed on the man before us.

"It's…it's…not possible!" he exclaimed.

"William! What's going—?"

He interrupted me before I could finish. "Leinad!" he whispered and pointed at the man.

"What?" I looked at the man once again.

The smiling gentleman gazed into my eyes with warmth and compassion, but I was not comforted. His features were familiar, but I was sure that William had lost his mind. This man was mature—a bit older than I—but he was certainly not the age of an old man. Leinad would be very old by now…many years older than when I last saw him. William still looked as though he had seen a dragamoth.

I stared hard at the man. "What is your name, sir, and how do you know ours?"

"Cedric, William…please don't be alarmed. It is I, Leinad."

In a moment my mind crossed over the barrier of reality and contemplated the possibility that this was indeed Leinad. My skin crawled with bumps from head to toe, and I felt the same shock William was exhibiting. His hand still gripped my arm.

I shook my head. "Impossible!" I exclaimed quietly.

"So it seems, Cedric," the man said. "But do remember where you are, my old friend. The King is a king of wonder, and so is His kingdom. I have waited to see you for many years. Will you greet an old friend?"

He offered a hand, and I could hardly force myself to take it. His hand was firm and full of life—the way it had been when I was a boy, when he sliced apples for me and told me grand adventure stories. I struggled with reason, doubt, and hope all at the same time.

"But how…?"

"It is the Life Spice, Cedric," he said with a smile. "Haven't you felt it already too?"

He was right. I had both felt and seen *something* in my fellow companions. It was part of the mystery I hadn't been able to identify but had attributed to the wonder of the new kingdom.

"The Life Spice restores and heals the body," Leinad said. "You saw it as a healing ointment when William was hurt, but its true form is the flowering plant that grows abundantly here in the kingdom. It is everywhere. In the water…in the air…in the food…everywhere. It is the King's way of bringing new life, even to the old."

Years ago, I had once thought Leinad was becoming delusional, but now it was I who appeared to be losing my mind. I stood motionless, gawking at this man whose hand I held, trying to make sense of it all.

"I do say, gentlemen, you look as though you've seen a ghost," he said with a smile.

William finally loosened his grip on my arm. "Leinad, is it really you?" he asked with excitement.

Leinad chuckled. "You never did quite believe me, William, but now I see in your eyes that you are first to accept the incredible as truth."

I began to recognize again all the characteristics of my old mentor in the face and voice of this vibrant man before me.

"Look around," he said. "The only aged people you will see are those who have just arrived from Arrethtrae."

We looked, and he was right. That was the other part of the mystery I couldn't put into words.

Leinad looked at me again. "Tell me, Cedric, have you ever seen an *old* Silent Warrior? How old do you think they are?"

I shook my head. "If this is true, sir, how…ah…young will you become?"

"The Life Spice does nothing magical, Cedric; it simply heals the body and restores all functions to full health. I am not becoming younger; my body is becoming stronger. The heart, lungs, muscles, bones, skin, and even the mind are restored to their perfect design. It is an exhilarating feeling! You have only just begun to experience it."

I paused to consider my own body and realized he was telling the truth. I had never felt better, and each hour that passed was better than the last. The ache in my left shoulder that I had learned to live with was less painful now than ever before.

"What of the children?" I asked, still trying to adjust to this concept.

"They will grow into adulthood slightly faster than usual but without any hindrances due to illness or injury. They too will experience a perfect body."

William and I both stood in silent contemplation. I looked over at him and could see that he believed our friend.

I smiled at my "old" friend and mentor. "Leinad, it is good to see you!" I opened my arms and embraced him. His strong arms wrapped around me.

"And you, my dear Cedric…and you, William!"

William and Leinad also embraced, and our surprise reunion became so joyful that I could not help the tears that welled up in my eyes. We talked briefly of many things. It was like having a dream of a lost friend, where you desperately try to squeeze every ounce of companionship from the passing moments before you wake. Finally, Leinad held up his hands to stop us.

"Cedric, William, we have forever! Let's not spoil our time in haste." He laughed, and I realized that it was the first time I had ever seen Leinad truly laugh. Oh, it was good to be home!

Something caught Leinad's eye, and his laughter stopped. A smile was on his lips, and adoration filled his eyes.

"Gentlemen, please allow me to introduce you to the companion of my heart…my wife, Tess!" He held out his left hand, and the sweet hand of a beautiful lady filled it.

I had only imagined what Tess might look like. Leinad had tried to describe her to me once, and I had imagined the woman who filled his stories, but my imaginary Tess was nothing like the lady who stood before us. Something in her delightful smile was familiar… *My Tess must have had the same smile,* I thought. What a noble woman she was. Her dark auburn hair hung loosely about her shoulders. Leinad seemed taken with her even now…perhaps every time they met. She looked even younger than Leinad, but I quickly realized that she had lived under the rejuvenation of the Life Spice much longer than he. In her eyes, though, I could see the wisdom of age.

William and I bowed, and she bowed her head in response.

"It is an honor for me to meet you, my lady," I said.

"And I, my lady," William said.

It felt like we were in the presence of two Arrethtraen legends.

"The pleasure is mine," said Tess. "I have heard much of your courage and devotion to spread the good news of the

Prince throughout the kingdom of Arrethtrae. On behalf of those who have gone before, thank you."

Her elegance and charm were unmatched when compared to any lady I had ever met, and yet she was thoroughly genuine.

"My lady, your words are humbling and too generous, I fear. It is because of you and Leinad that hope was given to us. Your mission was honorable unto all. On behalf of those who have come after, thank you."

She smiled and accepted my praise gracefully. She turned to Leinad and kissed his cheek. "Hello again, husband," she said quietly.

Their marriage in Arrethtrae had been cut short by her injury, and I never thought we might meet her. I imagined that the few years of reunion they'd had here were not nearly enough to recover what they felt they had lost. It brought joy to my heart to know that my old friend could receive with gladness that which he'd longed for but never dared believe possible. I remembered seeing his old form, sitting at the table in his cottage outside of Chessington. He would gaze out his window, looking south to the waters, dreaming of the Kingdom Across the Sea, longing for his Prince and his Tess.

I was able to find Rob, Barrett, and Cullen and introduced them to Leinad and Tess. The spirit of brotherhood within our small group was powerful.

I put my arm around William's shoulder. "What a day, my friend. What a glorious day!"

CHAPTER FOUR

MYSTERY'S KIN

 Leinad and Tess graciously invited me and many of my closest friends to their home the following week for a meal and fellowship. That allowed us enough time to settle in and partake in all the welcoming festivities that the King and the Prince had planned for Their people.

Beneath the sunlight of a pristine day, I walked with William to Leinad and Tess's palace.

"William, it seems that every day we are here something new surprises and delights us, does it not?"

"Indeed, Cedric," he agreed. "I feel like a child of a wealthy family at a continuous festival."

Even the streets were awe inspiring. Having experienced just a few days of this glorious kingdom, I couldn't imagine why the King cared at all about Arrethtrae. But I knew it was not the charm of the country, the beautiful streets, or even the magnificent city that swayed the heart of the King. It was the people. I had seen the King's deep love for the people firsthand through His Son, the Prince—a love so deep that He offered His only Son to save them. It is the people who make a kingdom great, but the King's love for them makes the kingdom even greater. I was realizing that these two kingdoms, both here and Arrethtrae, would forever be close to the heart of the King—not for their beauty but for the people within them.

William and I walked up the steps of a great palace. No guards were necessary. We were greeted at the doors by a large fellow I immediately recognized from the ship. He did not seem surprised to see me. The ship's crews of Silent Warriors had kept their distance from the Arrethtraen people during the voyage but were a bit more amicable since our arrival. I learned early on that Silent Warriors are extremely serious fellows.

"It is good to see you, Yutan," I said politely.

"And you, Sir Cedric."

"This is my good friend William."

The Silent Warrior bowed. "It is a pleasure to meet you, Sir William."

"And you, sir," William said.

"Sir Leinad and Lady Tess are waiting for you in the great hall."

"Thank you, Yutan," I said, and we walked in that direction.

As we approached the great hall, the sound of voices and laughter began to fill the hallway down which we walked. We entered the great hall through two massive oak doors that were open wide. Leinad and Tess were just beyond the entrance and greeted us warmly. Cullen and Keely, Barrett and his family, and Rob had already arrived. There were a dozen others; some I knew and some I did not. As we talked, Tess saw someone behind us and excused herself.

"So, Cedric," Leinad asked, "have you adjusted to life here yet, or does the wonder of this kingdom still confound you?"

"How does one adjust to paradise, Leinad?" I asked. "It seems to me that one must accept being surprised and delighted daily!"

"Speaking of delight"—Leinad smiled and looked beyond us—"here comes a delight of which I dared not dream."

We turned about to see Tess walking arm in arm with another beautiful lady.

"Leinad, look who has returned from a mission in time to join us for dinner this evening," Tess said, beaming.

Tess delivered the young lady to Leinad, who embraced her warmly. "Talea, I'm so delighted you could make it!" he said.

The surprise on my face must've been evident, for here before me stood the mysterious woman from the ship. I couldn't imagine what possible connection she might have with Leinad and Tess. Neither Arrethtraen nor Silent Warrior, she was an enigma that I resolved to find the answer to this evening.

Talea kissed Leinad on the cheek as they embraced. I thought the greeting a bit too friendly, but Tess did not seem to mind at all. I knew that Leinad had never spoken of this mystery lady before, so their acquaintance must have been made since Leinad's arrival here. And yet their affection for each other seemed to go deeper than friendship.

Talea held Leinad's hands and stepped back to look at him. "Father...it is so good to see you!"

At that, I nearly stumbled backward. *Talea—Leinad and Tess's daughter! How could this be?* Leinad delighted in welcoming his daughter—and in the shock on my face. "Cedric, you look almost as surprised as I felt when I learned of my daughter," he said with a grin. "Talea, allow me to introduce you to the young man to whom I passed the mantle of my hope. Cedric, please meet Talea, my daughter."

Talea turned to face me and smiled with the same sweetness I saw in Tess. I realized that I had recognized Tess's smile when I first met her only because I had first seen Talea. I tried to recover from what must have been a rather dumbfounded stare. Talea offered her hand this time.

"I am pleased to meet you, Sir Cedric," she said sweetly.

"And I am pleased to meet you, Lady Talea...again," I said, bowing and kissing the back of her hand. The fragrance of Talea's perfume rose from her wrist and lightly filled my nostrils with a sweet scent I knew I would never forget.

I rose up and felt some satisfaction in the questioning look upon Leinad's face.

"You have met before?" he asked.

"As a matter of fact, we have," I said. I let loose of her hand, and Talea glanced toward William. Leinad looked lost in thought, so I began the rest of the introductions.

"Talea, this is my good friend William—"

"Please forgive me," Leinad interrupted. "William, please allow me to introduce you to my daughter, Talea."

They exchanged courtesies, and Leinad returned to his question. "How is it possible that you two have met?"

I looked at Talea, but she seemed content to remain silent, so I spoke. "On our transport ship there was a mysterious young woman who was neither Arrethtraen nor a Silent Warrior. All of my attempts at discovering her identity failed, and she seemed to avoid me for most of the journey. Although you call her your daughter, I must admit that I am at a loss as to how this is possible."

Leinad laughed out loud. "Oh, what a coincidence that put you upon the same ship as Talea! I can imagine the awkwardness of it." He seemed to thoroughly enjoy the thought.

Talea looked a bit sheepish. "I am sorry, Sir Cedric, if you felt offended in any way. You see, I could not reveal my identity to you, nor could I lie. The wonder of the Life Spice had not been disclosed to you yet, and neither I nor any of the Silent Warriors were allowed to divulge anything of that nature while on mission. I spoke to you too much as it was, for your curiosity was great."

"There is no need to apologize, my lady," I replied. "But I must admit that I am still puzzled as to how you are Leinad's daughter."

Tess put her arm around Talea. "Talea is our one and only child, Cedric," she said warmly. "In Arrethtrae, I grew weak from my injury, and I was taken across the Great Sea to the Isle of Sedah. My departure from Leinad was hard to bear, but the Silent Warriors who came for me said I would soon die if I did not go with them. Leinad insisted, and I finally acquiesced.

What neither Leinad nor I realized was that I was with child. The voyage across the Great Sea nearly killed me, but once on the island, the Life Spice began to strengthen my body. Shortly thereafter, I found that I was carrying a baby." She smiled at Talea.

"I had a daughter and never knew it until I arrived on the island, Cedric," Leinad said. He put his arm around Talea and Tess. "Can you imagine the day of my reunion with my wife *and* my daughter?"

"But why were you taken to an island and not brought here to the kingdom?" I asked.

"No Arrethtraen was allowed into the kingdom until the Prince had completed His mission. When He died and rose again, He came to the Isle of Sedah and brought us into the kingdom." Leinad paused. "Only the Prince could unite us with the King. We all waited for Him. Even though I was not with you, I waited for the Prince as well."

I looked at Talea. "But those hideous creatures… Didn't you say they came from the caverns on the Isle of Sedah? How did you survive?"

"The island is divided by a mountain," she explained. "One side belongs to Lucius; the other was protected by Silent Warriors and became a place of refuge for us while we waited for the Prince. I saw the scynths only once before—there on that island. Yutan told me they abide deep in the mountain in caverns, and only Lucius can control them." She appeared unnerved. "I am glad to be here now."

Our group fell silent as we contemplated Talea's last bit of information.

Leinad finally spoke up to restore the festive mood. "Talea, after dinner you must challenge William and Cedric to a bout on the Intrepid Course. I think you might find your equal in one of them," he said with a sly smile.

From Talea's response, I could tell she had a competitive side that was no small part of her character. That had been evident even on the ship.

"Intrepid Course?" William asked.

"Yes," Tess answered. "While on the Isle of Sedah, the Silent Warriors mentored Talea and trained her in the art of the sword while I recovered. To condition her, they developed a challenging course that she loved to run. Over the years, as she grew, she began to beat even the Silent Warriors. The course tests not only strength, but stamina and speed."

"Don't even bother trying, gentlemen," a deep voice from behind us said. We turned to see Yutan smile admiringly at Talea. "You will save yourself a dose of embarrassment at the hands of this little lady if you refuse."

"Yutan, you let me win to make me feel good," Talea said jokingly.

"Yes…when you were just a lass, my lady. But I have not bested you in years and not for lack of trying, as you well know."

Talea laughed. "Yutan reconstructed the course here on our palace grounds for me. It was an important part of my childhood."

"Because of her skill," Yutan said, "Micalem has allowed Talea to accompany us on many of our sea missions. Take her challenge, but know that I have warned you."

William shook his head. "I think I shall leave my dignity intact and refuse. But thank you just the same."

Leinad looked at me with a raised eyebrow. I felt coerced, but thought it might afford me an opportunity to acquaint myself more with Talea.

"I humbly accept the challenge, provided Talea will be kind and not humiliate me too dramatically," I said.

Yutan slapped my back with a large hand. "Eat lightly, my friend, for though she is as pretty as a flower without, she is as tough as the largest of Silent Warriors within."

Shortly thereafter, Gavinaugh and Keanna arrived, followed by Sandon, Weston, Marie, Addy, and Keaton. Addy and Keely became instant friends, and Keaton was now old enough to hold his own with them.

It was good to see Gavinaugh, for I desired to talk with him but had not yet had the opportunity since our arrival. "Sir Gavinaugh, what a delight to see you. You look well." I offered my left hand to greet him, but he smiled and extended his right instead.

"What a pleasure to see you as well, Sir Cedric." He grasped my hand, and I felt the full strength of his grip.

"I see your thorn has been removed," I said, joyful for him.

"Yes, and I am stronger than ever. I can't tell you how good it feels to be whole again," he said. He formed a fist with his right hand and opened it. The injury he had received from the blade of a vicious Shadow Warrior had left his right arm use-less for years, but now it seemed completely healed. His eyes gleamed. Keanna joined us, and she slipped her arm in his.

"Good evening, Lady Keanna. I see that you have been made whole as well."

She smiled and leaned into Gavinaugh. "I'll never let him go again," she said, gazing at him with great admiration.

There were more introductions and light conversation before we were called to dinner. It was a marvelous meal and a time of pleasant fellowship. Taking Yutan's advice, I did not eat quite so much.

As the afternoon lingered, Leinad eventually brought us to the Intrepid Course on the far side of the palace grounds. It was a veritable plethora of obstacles and challenges that I had never before seen. There were ropes, trees, targets, beams, and even a rock cliff, which I imagined was to be scaled at some point in the run. I began to question my decision to accept Talea's challenge, or rather Leinad's. I had never pictured Leinad as a father. It was interesting to see the healthy pride of a father within him.

Leinad turned to the large Silent Warrior. "Yutan, in all fairness to Cedric, would you run the course first for him so that he is not at too much of a disadvantage?"

"Certainly, Sir Leinad," he replied.

Yutan removed his outer tunic, revealing well-sculpted muscles. As he ran the course, I concentrated on each task he performed. There were ropes to climb, beams to walk, pendu-lums to evade, arrows to shoot, and rocks to scale. At one point, he was required to retrieve a sword and strike three opposing targets in a specific sequence all within a certain amount of time. His sword moved quickly, but it took him two tries before he was rewarded with a drawbridge that automatically lowered in place to allow him to cross a wide ditch filled with water. It took some time before he completed it, and when he did, sweat ran profusely down his brow, neck, and torso. He finished the course by ringing a small bell at the end. While he was running the course, Talea had disappeared and returned adorned with the same outfit, minus the cape, that I had first seen her wearing on the ship. She looked fit for combat in an unusual way.

Talea came and stood before me with her fists on her hips. The sweet smile from before had been replaced with the stern face of a competitor. "Are you sure you want to do this?" she asked. The tone of a fierce challenge was in her voice.

"Lead the way, my lady," I replied.

We readied ourselves, and Yutan gave the word to start. I instantly became aware of a social dilemma. *How do I not look a fool and yet preserve the honor of Talea?* I entered the course with every intention of letting Talea win, but within minutes it became evident that "letting" her win would not be a problem. Although my strength was superior, her speed and agility were like that of a cat. She quickly maneuvered into the lead, and it took all I had to stay up with her. Before long, I was breathing hard and sweating like an overworked horse.

Talea seemed to move from challenge to challenge undaunted by physical strain. Partway through the course, I caught a second wind and started to feel the rhythm of the obstacles. I was closing on Talea, and the challenge of the competition soon took hold of me. Keely, who had been watching closely, found it an opportune time to cheer exuberantly for Talea.

Our leads were exchanged many times during the last half of the course. Talea became fiercer in her competitiveness, as did I. She edged forward just near the end with one obstacle remaining, and I knew I could not overtake her. After clearing the last obstacle, she glanced back toward me as I redoubled my efforts. We both stretched our hands for the rope of the bell, but she stumbled and missed. Without thinking, I grabbed the rope and pulled. I regretted it an instant later when I saw the hurt on her face.

Our audience politely applauded, and I reached to lift Talea to her feet. She hesitated but took my hand. I felt horrible. "I am sorry," I said quietly.

"Do not be sorry. You have won fairly. You deserve my congratulations."

"I am sorry you tripped. You were quite in the position to win," I said, trying to ease the tension and make both her and myself feel better. It did not seem to work.

"It appears we have a new Intrepid Course champion," Leinad said without much enthusiasm but with a genuine smile.

But there was no victory in the victory. I reminded myself that it was just a friendly competition, but I still felt miserable. Tess gracefully redirected all of us back to the palace for refreshments. Talea resumed her pleasant demeanor as she helped Leinad and Tess host their guests. Everyone seemed to thoroughly enjoy themselves except me.

Talea and I were polite to each other the remainder of the evening, but I felt a distance between us that I did not like and did not know how to close. It was the only sadness I had felt since arriving in the kingdom.

When William and I left, we walked in silence for a while. He finally placed an arm over my shoulder. "Your heart is good, my friend. She will see that with time."

"You are a good friend, William. Next time, please rescue me from my folly, lest I make a bigger fool of myself than I did this evening," I responded.

"You are no fool, Cedric, and there was little I could do for you. I do not think you would feel this way were it not for Talea."

I wasn't sure what he meant by his last comment, and I chose not to ask him. I was thankful for William. He knew me like a blood brother, and I hoped I was as good a friend to him as he was to me.

Some days later, I revisited Leinad and Tess's home, hoping to make things right with Talea, but she had departed on another sea mission with Yutan. I awkwardly apologized to Leinad, but he reassured me that all was fine. I could not convince myself of it though until I met with Talea personally. Unfortunately, it seemed that might not happen for a long time. But other matters helped occupy my mind and my time, for which I was thankful.

CHAPTER FIVE

THE AWAY
YEARS

 A few weeks passed, and as Knights of the Prince, we resumed our training once again. We knew that our reprieve from the clutches and effects of the Dark Knight was only a temporary respite. The Prince continued to teach us, train us, and prepare us for a future mission back in Arrethtrae. He brought our skill with the sword to a higher level of mastery. He was patient but did not allow complacency in any aspect of our training.

"Cedric, you have mastered the sword and all of the maneuvers I have taught you," the Prince said as He observed my training. "But now you must master your feet. When you encounter a Shadow Warrior, your footwork is what will save you. The sword and upper body will be ineffective if your legs and feet cannot carry you to a position of advantage quickly. Balance and speed start at the ground."

"Yes, my Prince," I replied and watched closely as He demonstrated.

When He finished, He looked intently upon me. "Life is good here, Cedric," He said and placed a hand on my shoulder. "In Arrethtrae, the threat of evil kept you on your guard, but remember this: the most dangerous threat of evil is when it seems to be absent."

I pondered His words and vowed not to forget them.

"Do not neglect your training, Cedric…here or in Arrethtrae, for the days of evil are not over!"

I was struck once again with the realization that the Prince was no ordinary man. It was as though He could see the future. His intelligence, discernment, and wisdom seemed to have no bounds.

During our absence from Arrethtrae, a time of great peril had come for all who remained. Their portion of anguish was doubled, for not only were they under the absolute, tyrannical rule of the Dark Knight, but the King's wrath against the people was great because they had rejected Him and the Prince.

Although none of the Knights of the Prince were allowed back to our beloved land during the years of peril, we learned much from the Silent Warriors' reports about the condition of Arrethtrae. Their role in the kingdom had changed once all of the Prince's Followers were taken. They had become observers instead of messengers, and implementers of the King's judgment instead of protectors of His people. Although I was joyful to be with the Prince again, I could not deny a heart that was heavy for the kingdom and for the people left behind, even though they had rejected the King. I wondered if I could have done something more.

The Dark Knight, Lucius, established total control of the kingdom under the name Alexander Histen. His rule was ruthless, and since all of the Knights of the Prince had been taken across the Great Sea, there was no one left to counter Lucius's reign of terror. The people of Chessington who remained were confused and beguiled. Unwilling to accept the Prince as the King's Son, they continued to look for a deliverer. Initially they wondered if Alexander Histen was he, but they quickly came to understand the treachery that followed in his wake. He established his throne in our beloved city of Chessington. It was the ultimate insult to the King, since this was the city and the chosen people through which the Prince would deliver those who followed Him.

Although the citizens of Chessington who remained rejected the Prince as the King's Son, they had not rejected the King or their belief in His promise of a deliverer. And although the King was grieved by their rejection of His Son, He did not abandon the people of Chessington forever. He knew they would eventually accept the Prince as their king in Arrethtrae. As the reality of Histen's treachery became obvious to the people of Chessington, they found themselves at enmity with two kingdoms and two kings: one glorious and good, the other evil and loathsome.

As their days of peril lengthened, the citizens of Chessington began resisting Histen's rule and his proclamation that he was the true king of Arrethtrae. Histen ruled all of Arrethtrae with a fierce hand. He demanded the allegiance of all and received it from all—all except the citizens of Chessington. Though intense persecution followed, they would not bend their knee to him. It was during this time of immense tribulation that the people of Chessington began to turn their hearts to the Prince. Some remembered the Prince and His profound words, while others listened to the stories and knew that they had misjudged the man…the deliverer. Now they wondered if there was any hope left. They felt the abandonment of the good King and the hatred of the evil one.

In the culmination of his anger and vengeance, Histen temporarily left Chessington to gather together a force of Shadow Warriors and Arrethtraen men so massive that no castle or fortress or city could stand for even an hour against its attack.

Now Histen wanted to utterly destroy Chessington and all of the King's people once and for all, for they were a reminder of the one he could not be—the one true King. Their only hope was to stand honorably against the coming onslaught of an evil army, even though it would mean certain death, for rule under Histen was not an option the King's people would accept.

Shortly after Histen left Chessington to gather his final forces of destruction, an assembly of the King's people gathered in the city square beneath the very tree upon which the Prince had died. A Silent Warrior named Gabrik had made a number of voyages across the Great Sea to report the condition of Arrethtrae to the King. Oftentimes, Gabrik's reports were given aloud at the King's grand palace courtyard for all the Knights of the Prince to hear. Upon his last return, he had recapitulated the words of Fenton at this assembly. Fenton was one of the men of Chessington responsible for turning the hearts of the people back to the Prince. I will never forget the impact his passionate words made upon the King. Through Gabrik we heard the words and saw the King's response:

"People of Chessington, our hands are red with the blood of the One who would deliver us! Only in this dark hour do we see our grievous mistake, for our King has rightfully abandoned us, and our sworn enemy has gone to gather an army to utterly destroy us. The truthful words of Leinad fell upon our fathers' deaf ears and hardened hearts, as did the words of the Prince upon our own. There is no promise left for us...no hope...no future. My soul is sick with grief at our betrayal, and yet within my bones I feel the zeal to make my life count for the King and His Son. Our final hour is come! Stand with me for the King and His Son against the evil one."

Gabrik spread his arms open wide as he recalled Fenton's final words to the people.

"Hope against hope do we call across the Great Sea. Oh my King, forgive us for our betrayal! We beseech You to incline Your heart to us one more time. Though we only deserve Your wrath and judgment, we appeal to Your kindness and mercy as King of all. Forgive us, oh King, and let us be Your people once again!"

Gabrik lowered his arms and bowed his head, and our assembly stood in silent contemplation before the King. A tear fell from the royal cheek of the King as He turned to face His Son.

"It is time!" the King proclaimed.

The Prince rose to His feet. "Silent Warriors and Knights of the Prince, prepare your hearts. We sail for Arrethtrae!"

The Silent Warriors drew their swords and lifted them high into the air. In unison they shouted, "The King reigns...and His Son!"

The Knights of the Prince drew their swords and echoed their cry, "The King reigns...and His Son!"

The Prince looked at Micalem, the commander of the Silent Warriors, and nodded.

Micalem turned to face his warriors. "Prepare the ships. Arrethtrae awaits her King!"

Under the majestic evening sky in the heart of the Kingdom Across the Sea, the distant cry of the people of Chessington had been heard, and the heart of a King was moved. 🔲

CHAPTER SIX

CHESSINGTON'S HOUR

We left the Kingdom Across the Sea and sailed back to Arrethtrae, where the massive and evil army of Lucius would soon be descending upon Chessington. Our force disembarked far enough southeast of Chessington to escape the attention of all. The journey to the hills east of the city was made at night under the protection of dark. The full moon was enough to light our way. Just beyond the crest of the near horizon lay the Chessington Valley. The Prince sent a small contingent of Silent Warriors to scout the approach of Lucius's army. By the time of their return, the direction of the deadly force was already evident by the rising dust cloud to the north where the higher lands of the plains were dry.

The voyage across the Great Sea and across the southern kingdom to this place has afforded me time to remember. And upon this trek I have shared the saga of this great kingdom with all who would listen, for its telling has changed the destinies of many people. But my time of reflection is over, and the future is unknown.

Once again, the Chessington Valley north of the city would host the battle of the ages, just as it had when Leinad and the Knights of Chessington faced Zane and his army many years before. As I scanned the horizon from left to right, my eyes came to rest on the line of gallant knights and Silent Warriors beside me that stretched as far as the eye could see. I saw Sir Gavinaugh, a brilliant sword affixed on each side of his belt—for now both arms were whole and skilled instruments of the King's judgment. There was also the mighty Leinad, whose eyes were fixed upon the Prince before us, now ready to give our orders.

"Silent Warriors and Knights of the Prince," the Prince said loudly for all to hear, "this is the day of deliverance for Chessington and all of Arrethtrae! Let your hearts be bold and your faith be sure, for I am with you. Today is the Day of Judgment for Lucius. His reign of tyranny is over. Today is the day of victory for freedom!"

The entire force of gallant knights raised their swords in silent celebration, for the shouts of thousands would carry too close to the ears of our enemy.

"Captains, approach," commanded the Prince. Dressed in full battle armor shining in the light of the early dawn, He exuded fierce power.

Micalem was already at His side. Gabrik broke from the ranks of the Silent Warriors, as did Leinad, Tess, Gavinaugh,

Keanna, Weston, William, and I. We joined the Prince to await our orders. Keef and Ramon were captains also, but were not present. I looked at the faces of my companions. All were experienced veterans of the sword and of battle. I was humbled and honored to be in their presence. From peasant boy to captain of the Prince's army, such noble company made me feel undeserving.

The Prince's eyes were confident, and His countenance was fiercer than I had ever seen it. "We will split our forces and surround the valley," He said. "We must maintain complete surprise. Five of our ships under the command of Keef and Ramon have disembarked west of the city and will travel north to cover the western ridge of the valley. Leinad and Tess, you will take your men into the city to reinforce the citizens of Chessington that have gone out to fight. Keep your men out of sight so that Lucius will not see any more than the force led by Fenton. You must take the brunt of the battle, for though Fenton's men are brave, they are ill-trained and inexperienced."

Leinad and Tess nodded in acknowledgment.

The Prince addressed Gavinaugh, Weston, and Keanna. "Take your men north along the eastern ridge of the valley. You will pass beyond Lucius's advancing forces. Your challenge will be to remain undetected for you are outnumbered and we will be too far away to help you. Once beyond their advance, circle behind their forces to block any retreat they attempt to the north."

The Prince turned. "Micalem and Gabrik will lead the main force from the east."

The Prince turned at last to William and me. He hesitated momentarily, and His face showed more concern than before. "Cedric, William, your mission is the most dangerous of all. We must lure Lucius into attacking before he is ready, and you must be that lure. They would recognize Silent Warriors even from a distance, so I have given this mission to you. Take twenty men and ride into the valley. First meet with Fenton and tell him that the King has heard his plea. Tell him that the return of the Prince is imminent. Then you will ride north, straight to the enemy. Lucius usually sends a small contingent of men in advance to be his eyes. You will engage those men long enough for Lucius to see it. Retreat down the valley, and Lucius will pursue. Then join Leinad and Tess on the outskirts of Chessington."

We nodded without hesitation. The Prince addressed us all. "When you hear the trumpet of Micalem, bring all of your forces to bear upon Lucius and his men—Shadow Warriors and Arrethtraens alike. We will have them surrounded on four sides. The day of mercy is over...the Day of Judgment has come!"

The Prince raised His magnificent sword above His head. "The King reigns!" He exclaimed.

"And His Son!" we replied. The Lion of the kingdom was to meet the dragon once again.

Our small circle dispersed, and we returned to the men. In a short time, our large force of Silent Warriors and knights was divided into three contingents. For my band, I chose twenty of the best fighters, which included my brothers Rob, Barrett, and Cullen. It was a difficult decision, because I knew this could be the mission that ended their lives. We rode to the ridge and gazed into the Chessington Valley once again. It was more beautiful than ever. It was hard to believe that this lush, serene valley would soon be host to the greatest battle in the history of two kingdoms. I was suddenly aware of the anxious feelings rising within my chest.

From this distance, Chessington looked as though it were peacefully sleeping in the dawn's cool morning air, but I knew that was a false perception. I'm quite sure that every remaining inhabitant was sick with fear and apprehension. I could just see Fenton's makeshift army at the northern edge of the city. Tiny figures peppered the green countryside—although sizable, this army would be discouragingly small in comparison to Lucius's. I was not allowed to reveal the Prince's plan to them; however, I was anxious to share my message. At the very least, it might give them some hope.

I glanced at William, also deep in thought, and wondered at the picturesque scene below. He looked my way and nodded.

"Let's ride, men," I commanded.

The closer we came to Fenton's army, the more distinct the forms became. Although twenty approaching men would not normally be a threat to any army, this one was visibly nervous and wary as we drew closer. Fenton and two hundred or so other men were mounted, but most of the force was not. Their weapons consisted of swords, axes, pitchforks, and a variety of other farming implements. I pitied their position but admired their courage, as it was clear they believed that today they would surely die.

We slowed our gallop to a canter to appear less threatening. Some distance out, I stopped the men.

"Noble men of Chessington," I called. "We look for the one called Fenton."

One man and two others broke from the force and approached cautiously. Twenty strides away, they stopped. The leader sat tall on his mount.

"I am Fenton. Are you friend or foe?" he asked in a brusque voice. He was an older man with the look of a gentleman. Wisps of gray highlighted his temples.

"We are friends," I said clearly. The tension on his face eased slightly.

"If that be so, then I am bound to warn you to leave this valley, for today Histen comes to destroy our city and our people."

"I am afraid we cannot do so, sir," I replied. "I have a message for you and the courageous people of Chessington."

Appearing somewhat bewildered, Fenton cocked his head to the left and squinted his eyes.

"The King has heard your plea, and the return of the Prince is imminent," I said.

Fenton lowered his voice. "Who are you, sir?"

"Stand strong, gentlemen, and prepare for battle!" I exclaimed. I kicked my horse and commanded the rest of my men to follow. We rode north at full gallop, up the Chessington Valley, directly toward the enemy. The flow of wind across my face and the pounding of the horses' hooves upon the ground helped to ease my growing apprehension. A hundred things could go wrong, and we were delivering ourselves into the teeth of the dragon.

I did not know how many men we would encounter in Lucius's advance contingent. The success of our lure would depend largely on how long we could hold them off without being killed. To my left and right were twenty of the best swordsmen in the entire kingdom—men I trusted with my life.

And today we would all trust our lives to one another and to the wisdom of the Prince.

We rode hard, and our mounts seemed to love the race. The air was cool and sweet. Near the end of the valley, we descended into a thick, low fog. Our legless steeds seemed to float across, leaving a swirling misty wake behind. The brisk morning air bit into my cheeks, and my eyes began to water. Eventually, the terrain lifted us out of the lowest portion of the valley, and Chessington fell behind and out of sight. The air warmed slightly. Ahead, we could see a thin cloud of dust kicked up by thousands of mounts, which meant that Lucius's army had left the higher plains.

After some time, I slowed the men, and we rode more cautiously. All eyes were on the horizon as the tension mounted. A thick grove of trees obscured our view, and we approached it carefully. Then we entered the trees and worked our way through to the other side. At the edge of the tree line, I stopped the men. Although the country was open, we could not see beyond the rise a few hundred paces before us.

I gathered my men around and spoke softly. "We must be getting close! William and I will ride to the ridge and try to spot the advance contingent. I hope to lead them into the trees. Stay out of sight until we return."

William and I exited the trees, and I heard Rob order the men to spread out and stay secluded. We moved as quietly as possible, now looking all around us rather than just ahead. I felt uneasy, as though we were entering the dragon's lair. We drew our swords and rode up to the ridge that separated us from a view of the unknown.

But before we could reach the ridge, an avalanche of riders crashed down on us. Fifteen Shadow Warriors broke the line of the ridge, and time seemed to stand still as we felt the forked tongue of the dragon reach out and smell our purpose. The stench of evil seemed to flow down the hill and envelop us. With our swords drawn and the armor of the Prince clearly visible, our frozen moment quickly shattered. One warrior disappeared in retreat while the others drew their swords and charged us explosively. There was no way of knowing just how far behind the rest of the army was, which caused me much anguish.

I did not need to speak a word to William. We turned and rode hard to the trees where our men were waiting. I quickly calculated the odds of victory against these brutes and considered our chances at least even. We entered the trees with our enemy in close pursuit. Rob had predicted our path and had split the men to flank the Shadow Warriors with a surprise attack. We continued our feigned flight until I heard Rob bark the order for attack. We turned back and engaged the leading warriors as Rob and the rest of the men closed in from each side. Our ambush and larger number put us at an immediate advantage.

The familiar sound of clashing swords filled the air, but it had been some time since I had felt the intensity of real battle. Fighting on horseback required extra skill, but the Prince had taught us well. The first Shadow Warrior fell, and I advanced on the next. One of my men took a flesh wound, and two others protected him. Soon the ground held the bodies of five Shadow Warriors, and those remaining fell into retreat.

"Shall we pursue?" Cullen asked.

I faced a conundrum. We needed Lucius's army to pursue, not just to be warned. Yet I did not know how far over the ridge they were.

"Yes, pursue!" I ordered and kicked my horse to lead the way.

The Shadow Warriors crested the ridge and disappeared. We soon arrived on the ridge behind them and found ourselves looking full into the fiery eyes of the dragon—Lucius's massive army. We pulled so hard on the reins of our horses that some of my men nearly fell backward. It was an ominous sight, and a body-wrenching fear swept over me. The talons of the dragon reached for us as we turned and pressed our steeds to their fastest speed.

Not daring to look back, my men exploded through the grove of trees and pressed straight on for Chessington. I finally turned and saw that the leading edge of the army had slowed to a cautious advance through the trees. This widened the distance between us, for which I was grateful. The size of Lucius's army was overwhelming, yet it dawned on me that I should have been as afraid of the first hundred warriors as I was of the next ten thousand, but it was not so—I think because I was afraid for not only myself, but for all the people of Chessington as well. I hoped the Knights of the Prince and the Silent Warriors were ready for the ferocious army that charged behind us.

The lower Chessington Valley and its beautiful city came into view. As we neared Fenton's army, his men seemed to panic, for the valley behind us was filling with the advancing dark army of Lucius.

My knights rode straight to Fenton and gathered around him.

"What have you done?" he asked with a voice that carried the fear he felt.

"I have done the bidding of the Prince, Fenton. Settle your men, and prepare them to protect the city."

Lucius's army was just minutes away as they advanced unhindered upon the apparently helpless city of Chessington. The pounding of hoofbeats was broken only by the penetrating sound of one lone trumpet—Micalem's.

Behind Fenton's forces, the streets of the city came alive as Leinad and Tess ordered the advance of their men. I pointed to our forces as they moved forward through Fenton's men to join us.

"The battle belongs to the Prince!" I exclaimed.

Fenton turned and saw only a portion of his city's deliverance. Lucius's army was nearly upon us, and I felt the hot breath of the dragon as its jaws opened to devour us.

Fenton shouted above the noise of thousands of advancing horses. "May the Prince live forever, sir, and may our hearts be ever His, but even this is not enough to overcome the onslaught of Alexander Histen." Fenton looked at me with a mixture of hope and fear in his eyes as our men gripped their swords and weapons tightly and readied themselves.

I swept my sword across the valley's eastern and western horizons. "Look to the hills, from where comes your help!"

The valley horizons filled with the powerful forms of thousands of Silent Warriors. Lucius's men hesitated as they became aware of their impending demise. Keef and Ramon and their men were to the west; Micalem and Gabrik and their men to the east. Gavinaugh, Keanna, and Weston were positioning their men to the north behind Lucius's army. Leinad and Tess joined us with thousands of fellow knights, and we ordered Fenton to retreat to the city's edge. We positioned our men, and I beheld the unfolding of the battle of the ages. Leinad, Tess, Gavinaugh, Keanna, Weston, William, Rob, Barrett, Cullen, Keef, Ramon, Micalem, Gabrik, and countless courageous others all joined in one final battle to end the evil reign of Lucius once and for all. My fear was gone, for we all belonged to the Prince, and I was in the company of legends and heroes.

The sound of thundering horses faded to silence, and I sensed fear in the heart of the dragon. Now but a few hundred paces away, I still could not see individual faces, but one figure at the front stood out from the rest. He broke from his warriors a short distance and circled his horse a number of times. He was looking for someone. From the city behind us, Fenton's men and our men parted to allow the approach of a single rider. The Prince rode forward to where Leinad, Tess, William, and I were positioned. I felt insignificant but empowered next to Him.

Lucius stopped his horse when he recognized the majestic form of the Prince before him. There across the small expanse that separated these age-old foes, the fury of a fallen, jealous warrior met the judgment of a perfect King. The pain and anguish of many generations was heaped upon the ground between them, all because of the pride of one powerful warrior.

Lucius burst forth with a battle cry that swept through his men, and they charged full upon us. The Prince was unaffected and drew His magnificent sword, and Micalem blew his trumpet once again as the King's army advanced to slay the dragon. The Prince led the charge, and we followed. The distance between our forces diminished to nothing as the clash of thousands of swords and a thousand battle cries filled the air. The Prince focused only on Lucius, for no other dared face Lucius's sword. I concentrated on each adversary but was intently aware of the duel of masters next to me. Lucius's and the Prince's swords flew with blinding speed, but the Prince was the master of all…including Lucius. How he thought he could ever overcome the Prince was evidence to the power of his pride. There had been only one outcome from the beginning, and Judgment Day was here.

Within moments, Micalem and Gabrik engaged from the

east; Gavinaugh, Weston, and Keanna from the north; and Keef and Ramon from the west. The enveloping army of truth and justice swallowed up the dragon. I could see panic sweep through the Shadow Warriors and Lucius's Arrethtraen loyalists.

For most, the fight eventually moved from the backs of horses to the ground, where one's sword was more stable and sure. My current adversary was weakening, and I stole a moment to look to the Prince. Both He and Lucius had removed their helmets to allow for better vision. Though hatred spewed from Lucius toward the Prince, Lucius could not defend against the perfection of His sword. The Prince pounded each strike upon Lucius until there was a gap in his guard. The Prince then seized the opportunity and sliced the sword across Lucius's face, which left a long cut from the corner of his eye to his chin. The perfect, unscarred complexion of the Dark Knight was no more. Lucius stopped and reached for his face and saw his blood spill through his fingers. The fury in his eyes erupted through his sword, but it was small in comparison to the judgment wrath of the Prince—justice for all the murder, the pain, and the destruction to the kingdom and to the people empowered the Prince's arms. He gave Lucius no opportunity to yield honorably.

Lucius attempted an ad-vance and a thrust at the Prince, but the Prince easily countered a circling slice that would have split any other adversary in two. Lucius was able to retreat just enough to escape with a nonfatal gash across his chest. The Prince stared with fiery eyes at the Dark Knight, and I saw Lucius's pride succumb to a moment of sheer terror. I think that only now, after generations of time, did he grasp the complete and total supremacy of the Prince over him. The realization was temporary, however, and his hate-filled countenance returned.

William and I remained close, watching each other's backs, as did Rob and Barrett. Many comrades lay on the ground, but I did not see any who were dead. Many were injured, however, and I hoped the Life Spice within them would keep them well. The injured fell back and were replaced by others. We were nearby to Leinad and Tess and saw the mastery of their skill with the sword. It was an honor to fight for the King and the Prince next to such legends as these!

As the battle progressed, it became apparent that our victory was only a matter of time. It was a battle with a sure end. I advanced on another of Lucius's Arrethtraen loyalists, but he backed away in retreat with his free hand forward. He did not yet dare lay his sword down. Many of us were receiving the same response from even the Shadow Warriors. The only real fight left was that between the Prince and Lucius.

Lucius could not yield, for the pride of his past would not let him. At one point, Lucius charged upon the Prince in a careless attack. The Prince parried the reckless thrust and

could have easily run the Dark Knight through, but He didn't. Lucius's momentum took him close to the Prince. In one swift move, the Prince stepped aside and struck Lucius in the head with the pommel of His sword. Lucius collapsed to the ground—motionless. The fight was over, and so was the battle, for when Lucius fell, the will of his army was broken. The forces of the dark army began to drop their swords until the sound of clashing steel was no more.

The eyes of every man fell upon the Prince—both enemy and ally.

Micalem raised his sword in triumph. "Behold, the King of Arrethtrae has come!" he proclaimed and then knelt before the Prince.

As was foretold, every knee bowed down and proclaimed that the Prince was now King of Arrethtrae—from Silent Warrior to Shadow Warrior to every Arrethtraen. The Prince stood alone and welcomed the proclamation, for it was His Father's will. In my heart I knew that this was the beginning of an era to which even the days of Quinn could not compare, for every fiber of our King was true and noble. Power could not corrupt Him, for He already had all power and yet remained pure. I did not see pompous arrogance in Him as He stood the proclaimed King of Arrethtrae. No...I saw the restored joy that you see only on the face of a father whose child has been safely returned to him. The peace in the Prince's heart flowed out to the people, and those who loved truth and justice were comforted. Those who did not were ashamed.

Shortly after the people had accepted the reality that true

victory was won, the city of Chessington rose up with shouts of adoration and praise for their new King. Fenton led his men and the rest of the city in a victory celebration as they welcomed the Prince as King of their city and of Arrethtrae. It was a celebration of the ages to end the battle of the ages, for only now could the King's people enjoy the fulfillment of complete restoration through the Prince.

CHAPTER SEVEN

RETURN TO CAMELOT

The Prince ordered that all the injured be treated. The Dark Knight and the Shadow Warriors were gathered together under the guard of the Silent Warriors and taken away to the prison pits in a distant place called the Wasteland. The rest of the enemies of the King were given an opportunity to swear their allegiance to the new King of Arrethtrae. Those who did so were released to return home without weapons, and those who did not were eventually taken to the prisons of Daydelon in the land of the Kessons.

The news of the battle at Chessington and Lucius's defeat spread quickly through the kingdom. The few remaining forces of the Dark Knight dispersed and became a challenge for us to find. Nearly every city welcomed the Prince as King with open arms—some out of joy and some out of fear. The daunting task of restoring truth, justice, and honor to the kingdom lay before us. I could not even begin to know how the Prince was going to accomplish it, for you cannot order a heart to change, and many hearts were still inclined to do evil. Many were joyful and desired the peace that the Prince wanted to give them. But many struggled, for even though they wanted to change and embrace good, they had lived so long under the evil rule of Lucius that it was hard for them. Some harbored rebellious and evil hearts and did not want to change at all. They still loved Lucius and his wicked ways. Unfortunately, these people were also very deceptive and difficult to root out.

A few days after the great battle, the Prince called His knights before Him on the palace grounds of Chessington. The palace—and the entire city of Chessington for that matter—had fallen into a state of disrepair. The palace, the city, and the people had been abused and mistreated for many years during Lucius's reign. Now it was time to rebuild, restore, and reclaim all that had been taken under his tyrannical rule. There amidst the partial ruin of the palace stood the Noble One, unperturbed by the formidable task of renewing an entire kingdom. We gathered in silence as He looked over us and beyond, to the future of His people.

"My gallant knights, from this day forward Arrethtrae will be a kingdom of peace and prosperity once again." His penetrating eyes fell upon us, and His regal form seemed immovable. "You will be My arms of justice; you will be My arms of compassion. Together we will restore Arrethtrae to the perfection it was before the Dark Knight's shadow of evil fell upon the land. You have been faithful…you have been loyal…now you will reign with Me!

"Sir Leinad and Lady Tess, Knights of the Prince, to you is given the city of Daydelon. Rule with hearts of wisdom and with the courage the King has relied upon in times past.

"Sir Gavinaugh and Lady Keanna, Knights of the Prince, to you is given the region of Namor and the seas of the south.

"Sir Weston of Cresthaven, Knight of the Prince, to you is given the city of Thecia in the heart of the kingdom.

"Sir William of Chessington, Knight of the Prince, to you is given the region of the United Cities of Cameria.

"Sir Rob of Chessington, Knight of the Prince, to you is given Kroywen, first city of the United Cities of Cameria.

"Sir Barrett of Chessington, Knight of the Prince, to you is given the city of Chandril.

"Sir Cullen of Elttaes, Knight of the Prince, to you is given the city of Elttaes, second city of the United Cities of Cameria.

"Sir Gunther of Norwex, Knight of the Prince, to you is given the city of Norwex…"

And thus was given rule of all the regions and cities to the Knights of the Prince. The Prince looked at the knights as He gave them their reigns. I waited and listened, but no assignment was given to me. Did the Prince see something in me that might inhibit my ability to rule a city or a region? I rejoiced with each of my companions but admittedly was downhearted, for I felt as though I must have failed my Prince.

"Sir Deidrik of Canterbury, Knight of the Prince, to you is given the city of Canterbury.

"To all of My city prefects and regional governors, rule

with wisdom, compassion, and diligence, for you are My eyes, you are My arms, and you are My lips. Stay true to the Code!"

My heart was broken, until the Prince paused and looked directly at me. His gentle smile warmed me, and I found contentment in His gaze.

I will gladly be a servant in the house of my Lord rather than rule a city, I thought.

"To Cedric of Chessington, Knight of the Prince"—He paused, and I wondered if each knight had felt as I did when the Prince looked upon me. The strength in His eyes seemed to flow into my heart—"I give the role of ambassador to all of the kingdom of Arrethtrae. From Chessington, Cedric will deliver My words and My missions to all."

I lowered my head in gratitude, embarrassed at my previous feelings of self-pity.

A moment later, we all knelt in unison before our King of Arrethtrae. I am sure each of us felt honored and undeserving of the authority the Prince had entrusted to us. We resolved in our hearts to fulfill our responsibilities as knights beholden to the Code.

"Rise up, My knights," said the Prince. "Prepare yourselves to go forth and deliver the peace and prosperity I have desired for this land from the beginning. Take to the people that which restores."

The Prince held up a flowering plant of the Life Spice. "Take the Life Spice to all the people. Plant it in your cities and in your valleys and in your hills. Fill the kingdom so that all may be healed and restored. The days of sickness and pain are gone. From this day forth, Arrethtrae will be a kingdom of peace, prosperity, and good health!"

Many knights did not receive the authority to rule a city or a region. Some were assigned as guards to the prefects or regional governors. And the Prince warned us that some regions would not welcome His rule.

Later that day, the Prince walked with me among the remains of the once beautiful gardens of the palace.

"My King, I am unworthy of the noble mission You have given me... I do not even know how to begin," I said, feeling humbled.

He placed an arm around my shoulder. "Cedric, you are more than able. The mission is difficult because your travels will take you throughout the kingdom, but I have the utmost confidence in you. I need you to help My knights establish their rule. For the time being, I have assigned a contingent of men to be your escort. There is still danger."

We paused in our walk, and He turned to face me.

"Where do I start, my Lord?" I asked.

"I want you to travel with the knights who go to the United Cities of Cameria and establish My rule in that region. From there you will know where to go." He smiled as He read my lack of self-confidence.

"I have assigned a fellow knight to assist you...one with skill and discernment that I have not found in any other."

I was pleased and relieved. I would have hoped for William, but his duty lay in Cameria. "Who is he, my King?"

"The knight arrives by ship this evening. The *Valiant* will dock before sunset." The Prince resumed walking. We arrived at a spot that looked over the once majestic city of Chessington. I saw the ruin, but I knew He saw the potential splendor.

The Prince smiled. "Ah Cedric, it is good to be here. My beloved city will be beautiful once again, and the people will find the goodness they have sought for so long."

I tried to imagine what He saw but knew that my picture must pale in comparison to the one in the mind of the King.

I arrived at the docks south of Chessington late in the afternoon to wait for the arrival of my companion. I wondered who the Prince had chosen and if I knew him. Many ships arrived carrying supplies for Chessington, and the *Valiant* was among them. The crew began unloading the cargo, and I immediately recognized the slender form of Talea overseeing the operation. She was occupied with her task and did not seem to notice me, which was fine because I felt entirely awkward around her anyway. There are certain moments in our lives that we wish we could erase, for the embarrassment we live with is uncomfortable. Although Talea was a fascinating woman, she reminded me of such a moment, and I found it difficult to get past it. Yutan was beside her, as usual, helping organize the shipment.

I waited for the passengers to disembark. Three gentlemen exited the ship and walked toward the city without any hesitation in their step. After some time, I boarded the *Valiant* and sought out her captain to inquire of my assistant. As I approached, he hailed me first.

"Sir Cedric, I assume you have come to welcome your assistant?"

"Yes, Captain. Can you tell me where he is?"

He looked a bit puzzled and then smiled as though a thought entered his mind. "If you can be a bit more patient, I will help you in just a moment."

By now the unloading of the cargo was complete, and the captain called for Yutan. They had a short discussion to which I was not privy. I began to wonder if something was amiss. The two Silent Warriors approached me.

"Sir Cedric, I am sorry for the delay, but Yutan will assist you," the captain said and returned to his duties in his cabin.

"Yutan, it is good to see you." I reached out my hand. For some strange reason, I felt as though I had also offended Yutan that day I unintentionally insulted Talea back at Leinad's home, for his demeanor toward me was a bit cool. He obviously felt an obligation to Talea. I had perceived that his role for her was one of personal guard. Perhaps Leinad had asked him to watch over her? I could only guess.

"The captain tells me you are here to receive your assistant," he said brusquely.

"That is correct," I said, wondering why Yutan was charged to aid me with the matter.

Just then Talea approached. I took a deep breath and bowed slightly. "Lady Talea, I am honored to see you again."

She responded by nodding slightly. "It has been some time, Sir Cedric. What brings you to the *Valiant*?"

She stood tall and poised. A tousle of hair had come loose

from her braid and hung down the left side of her face. The ever-present air of competence hung about her. I was momentarily taken by her eyes and wondered what mission of adventure she would soon be upon. She caught my gaze and wiped away the loose bit of hair, tucking it behind her ear.

"I am here on business, my lady," I replied. "I am here to—"

Yutan interrupted. "I am told that the Prince has chosen Sir Cedric to be his ambassador to all of Arrethtrae," he said to Talea, almost bragging on me.

I was surprised and embarrassed by his comment. I turned my head away.

"Impressive..." Talea looked at Yutan strangely.

"I fear it is a task I am ill-equipped to handle on my own," I said, trying to recover some humility. "I am here to receive my assistant, whom the Prince has assigned."

Now it was Yutan's turn to look embarrassed. He looked away to the sea. Talea's poise turned into a look of confusion.

"You must be mistaken, Sir Cedric, for we do not carry such a man on the *Valiant*... Perhaps the *Dauntless* delivers the man you seek. She is due to dock after we depart." Talea looked at me and smiled briefly.

Now I truly was bewildered, for the Prince Himself had sent me to the *Valiant*. I did not respond but silently contemplated what had gone wrong.

Yutan turned back to Talea. "My lady," he said, "I must ask your forgiveness for not informing you earlier... Cedric comes for you."

I was as shocked as Talea looked. "I…but…that is not what I…"

"There is some mistake, Yutan," Talea said matter-of-factly.

"Yes, surely there is some mistake," I chimed in, then quickly regretted speaking it as I caught Talea's cold gaze.

Yutan looked at the deck. "There is no mistake, my lady. The Prince has chosen you to be Cedric's assistant. Your mission now lies in the heart of Arrethtrae. I will miss you."

"Excuse us," Talea said as she grabbed Yutan's arm and turned away from me. They walked to the end of the deck in serious discussion.

This was not at all what I had expected. The color of my mission had changed dramatically in an instant. It wasn't that I didn't like Talea, but I certainly was not comfortable with her…especially as an assistant. It seemed quite clear, however, that she did not like me, and that made things even more challenging. I did not relish the idea of becoming a despised authority.

I looked over at Talea and Yutan. Their words were intense at first, but as the reality of the situation sank in, Talea visibly softened toward Yutan. She stared down in silence and then looked up at him. I saw her quickly wipe away a tear and then embrace her large friend. She stepped back and resumed her confident posture.

As they returned to me, I tried to appear indifferent, as though I were receiving the knight I had expected.

"I will gather my belongings," she said and quickly walked past me.

Yutan and I stood in silence for a moment. "Take care of her, Sir Cedric," he finally said. "She has been like a daughter to me."

"I will protect her with my life, Yutan."

He smiled and we shook hands, and in that moment there passed a silent transfer of responsibility. "I know you will, and she will do the same for you. That is what worries me..."

CHAPTER EIGHT

PERIL AT LAKE PENSING

 Talea and I left the ship and boarded a small carriage that awaited us. She traveled light—just one small satchel—and I was pleased about that. The silence between us was awkward. I hadn't been expecting her as my assistant, and she hadn't been expecting such a drastic change in her mission for the King.

"It is good to see you again, Talea," I said, trying to be cordial.

"And you," she replied without looking my direction. It was not an enthusiastic reply by any means, but it was not indifferent either. Sitting across from me, she gazed out the window at the streets of Chessington as we traveled north toward the palace. I knew life had just taken a drastic turn for her, and she was trying to adjust. Talea was a stunning woman in both beauty and character, but any initial attraction I'd had to her was quickly dying with each encounter. I was about to ask her how she had been, but she cut through my attempt at casual conversation and pressed right to business.

"What is the purpose of our mission, and how long will it last?" She turned and finally looked at me for the first time since leaving the ship. For one brief moment, I thought I saw an expression of kind fellowship, but it was fleeting and the look of a professional warrior replaced it from that moment on.

I cleared my throat. "Initially, we are to help the newly selected city prefects and regional governors establish their governments. Once that is complete, which I am sure will take a fair amount of time, we are to represent the Prince and deliver His commands to the cities and regions as well as keep Him updated on the kingdom's progress." I looked at her briefly and then gazed out the carriage window myself. "As to the length of the mission or your assignment, I simply have no idea."

"I see," she said.

I looked back at her, and she stared blankly at me. I knew that I must clear any misconceptions from her mind and try to get us back on the right foot.

"Lady Talea, we are going to be working together for quite a while, and I am committed to fulfilling my duty to the Prince. Just to be up front with you, I didn't request you, nor did I know you were the one selected as my assistant until Yutan told us both on the ship. I'm sorry that you were surprised by it, but we have a job to do, and it's not going to be an easy one. If I've offended you in any way, I apologize. Let's respect each other and get on with our business."

She looked at me a bit less coolly and nodded. "Agreed."

Our relationship would remain purely professional, I was sure of that. It was painfully clear that she wanted nothing more to do with me than to accomplish our mission. I was not completely sure why she was so stoical toward me, but I accepted it and appreciated her abilities and planned to use them effectively in our dealings within the kingdom. Talea was charming…just not to me. And it was probably fortunate, because our businesslike relationship allowed me to focus completely on our mission and duty for the Prince rather than on civilities.

It took a number of days to prepare for our departure to Cameria. Five city prefects, one regional governor, and six contingents of knights made for a fairly large force of armed warriors. Additionally, Barrett and his men traveled with us as far as Chandril, where he was to rule.

We mounted, and I looked at William, Rob, and Barrett to my right. I smiled as I remembered our adventures together. They smiled, as if also remembering. Talea rode to my left, and Cullen and Keely, along with the other two city prefects, were beside her. I was amidst warriors on a noble mission, and I was honored to be with them.

"Lead on, Sir Cedric," William said with a broad smile.

"The honor is yours, Governor." I bowed from my mount.

He smiled and then sat tall on his steed. "Move out!" he commanded, and we launched into the kingdom on a mission of restoration.

As we rode, we talked of our missions and our new responsibilities. I sensed uneasiness in all but Cullen. His wholehearted ambition to serve the Prince seemed to overcome any lack of self-confidence, which was an encouragement to all of us. Cullen was an excellent addition to our company. If there was any apprehension in him, it was due to not knowing what had happened to family members he left behind.

I did not mind the length of our journey, because at its end William and I would part ways, and I was saddened at the thought. I knew no other kindred spirit like him, and I did not relish saying good-bye.

After many miles and much conversation, I realized that Talea had remained quiet through it all. I glanced her way, and William followed my gaze.

"Talea," William addressed her. "You have a rather challenging task ahead of you since Cedric here seems to find trouble wherever he goes. You must do your best to keep him out of it."

Talea smiled at him. "I'm sure it will be challenging indeed." She quickly resumed her quiet demeanor.

I glanced at William, and he raised an eyebrow. I shrugged and thought how much she reminded me of most of the Silent Warriors…only prettier and smaller. Keely maneuvered her horse next to Talea and found a friend there, for which I was grateful.

At Chandril, we left Barrett and his men and traveled northeast. We rode many days and finally arrived in the region of Cameria. It was a green and lush land with many forests and lakes. From the moment we arrived, I sensed greater apprehension in Cullen. This was unusual for a man of his confidence and caliber. He was obviously concerned about his family, but in addition, this land was his home, and he knew, as we all did, that his people had suffered greatly under the Dark Knight.

Most of the citizens welcomed us with open arms, both within the cities and without. They had tasted the evil deeds of Alexander Histen, Lucius's pseudonym for his role in Arrethtrae, and had been severely oppressed. Only those who had enjoyed positions of power and authority from Lucius resisted, and they were quickly routed, for Lucius and most of the Shadow Warriors were now in the prisons of the Wasteland. As is the case with all tyrannical, oppressive governments, only the leaders had prospered. This was clearly evident on the weary faces of the people and in the dilapidated condition of most of the cities' streets, shops, and homes.

The knights who accompanied the prefects were given leadership positions, but I also encouraged each prefect to find trustworthy and respected citizens and assign them to positions of authority. The knights' jobs were not just to rule but also to gain the trust and respect of the people. In each city, the Code was reaffirmed as the principle doctrine to govern each heart.

William traveled to each of the cities since he would ultimately be responsible for the entire region. Only one city remained: Elttaes. We had been delayed at Kroywen since it had been the largest and the most difficult in which to establish the new rule. It was also where William chose to reside because of its centrality to the other four cities. Cullen and his men departed for Elttaes before we were ready to leave Kroywen. He was anxious to return to the city to discover what fate his family and friends had endured. Unfortunately, no city, village, or farm had been spared the treacherous deeds of Lucius or his evil men. But I was not too concerned for Cullen—he was from this region, and we had thus far been well received. I said my farewells to Rob, and then William, Talea, and I and our twenty-five men rode on to Elttaes, nearly a day behind Cullen.

Elttaes was more than a day's journey away, so we set up camp that evening near Lake Pensing. The next morning as the men broke camp, William and I walked together, enjoying the vibrant beauty of the lake and forest and each other's fellowship.

"Well Cedric," William said with a smile, "did you ever imagine that two poor fishermen like us would ever find such adventure in life?"

I laughed. "My biggest dream as a young man was to own a fishing boat, but now we are joint heirs to an entire kingdom." I shook my head, still not quite believing it all. "Only a child would dare to dream of such things, my friend."

"Do you remember our willow-stick swords that we fought with to save the maiden in distress?" he asked.

"Yes…along the banks of the river near Leinad's home…" I could almost make myself believe I was there.

William and I walked onto a large jagged rock outcropping that extended a few paces into the crystal-clear waters of the lake. As a boy I would have loved to jump from it and into the cool water below. We stopped and soaked up the beauty of the lake. The shadows began to shorten, and the morning song of a variety of birds was sweet to hear. It was a quiet moment of total contentment—a moment infringed upon only by the realization of our near future. Both William and I knew that our time together was short. For the first time in our lives, we would be separated. As we looked far across the lake, I knew we both ached.

"You have been more than a brother to me, William," I said, though I could not look at him. "You helped me find hope when it was difficult to do so."

William did not face me either, but spoke to the lake. "Your friendship is more to me than life itself, Cedric. You have been my compass of wisdom… I will miss you more than I can say."

I finally turned and placed a hand on his shoulder. He placed his hand on my forearm, and the powerful bond of brotherhood that only two Knights of the Prince could feel passed between us.

"Cedric. William." I heard Talea's voice call from a short distance away in the forest behind us.

"This way," I called back.

Talea joined us on the outcropping and spent a moment taking in the beauty of the lake. The seriousness of the mission disappeared from her countenance, and her eyes sparkled like a child's.

You are still a mystery to me, Talea, I thought.

She broke her gaze and turned to me. "The men are nearly ready."

"Very well… We will depart for Elttaes immediately," I replied.

Talea turned her head slightly as if to listen for something.

"What is it, Talea?" William asked quietly.

"We are being watched," she said in a whisper.

We inconspicuously began searching our surroundings. Except for the lake before us, trees obscured our view in all directions.

"There!" William exclaimed in a hushed tone as he pointed toward some trees off the lakeshore. We followed his finger and saw the slightest bit of motion receding into the trees and over a rise in the forest. We drew our swords and pursued. I was amazed at Talea's sense of awareness.

"Was it a person or an animal of some sort?" I asked as we ran through the trees.

"I couldn't tell," replied William.

"It is a person," Talea said.

We made it to the rise in terrain and stopped to regain sight of our fleeing spy. Talea took off again slightly left of our original course, and we too saw the occasional movement that was broken by the trees before us. We pursued for some distance until we came upon a small hut that was nestled in a quiet recess of the forest. We approached cautiously, scanning the surroundings for any sign of danger.

"Is anyone here?" I called, supposing that at the most only two or three could live in such a small hut. I did not relish the thought of entering the hut, for not everyone in the kingdom was yet a friend of the Prince. And who was to know if all of the Shadow Warriors had truly been imprisoned? There was no reply.

"It looks abandoned to me," William said.

I looked at Talea, but she made no comment. She was studying the house intently.

"We will investigate, but be careful," I said and moved toward the door.

We entered the small hut. Though hardly livable, it was immediately apparent that someone had occupied it for some time. Talea and I investigated a larger room while William entered a smaller room off to our left. Our swords were drawn, and we were on full alert. A moment later I heard William speaking softly. We moved toward the open doorway.

"It's all right, miss. We are not here to harm you," William said.

A frightened young woman stood in the corner of the room with her hands clenched about the handle of a long-knife—which was pointed at William. Her eyes darted toward us as we entered and then back to William. Her fear was stark, and I pitied her. She was frail and thin and probably quite attractive, but fear and malnutrition had robbed her of her beauty. She was breathing hard and looked as if she was at the end of her strength. Talea and I approached no further as William tried to assuage her apprehension.

"Please put the knife down… We want to help you." William spoke in soothing tones.

"I don't believe you… You killed my father. Get away!"

"We did not kill your father, miss. We are…"

"All of Histen's men are murderers—stay back!" she yelled.

William was four paces away. He slowly sheathed his sword.

"I promise I will not hurt you," he said, showing his empty hands as he inched closer. He suddenly froze though when the woman turned the knife and pressed its deadly blade against her own abdomen.

"I will not let you torture me too!" she said in a panicked voice.

William held up his hands. "We are not Histen's men. We are Knights of the Prince. We have come to help you, not hurt you! Please don't harm yourself!"

The woman hesitated as she tried to process William's words. "You are lying! There are no Knights of the Prince in Arrethtrae—they were all taken away, and we were left to suffer under Histen!" Tears began to fill her eyes. "My sister...my brother. They left us here...to die!"

 William inched a little closer. "No, that is not true. The Prince has come back, and Histen is defeated. Look...look at my breastplate. It is the mark of the Prince, not Histen!" William said passionately. "Give the knife to me, and I will show you that what I speak is true."

The woman was obviously struggling between fear and hope. She seemed to want to believe but did not dare. She glanced at me, then at Talea. Talea smiled reassuringly, and the woman's face softened slightly, teetering on the edge of hope.

William resumed his careful motion toward the woman. "It's all right... Put the knife down, and I will get some food and water for you," he said tenderly. William was now only a pace away, and the woman's grasp on the knife relaxed. Exhausted, she yielded herself to what likely seemed an uncertain fate. She allowed William to place his hand on hers and pull the knife away from her body, all the while staring into his eyes. She peered at him, as if waiting for an evil transformation of his kind face, but she did not see it. Reassured, she collapsed. William caught her in his arms, and she melted into his embrace, incoherent and nearly unconscious. Her journey through the years of tribulation was over.

CHAPTER NINE

THE COST
OF FREEDOM

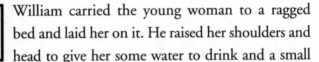 William carried the young woman to a ragged bed and laid her on it. He raised her shoulders and head to give her some water to drink and a small bit of cornmeal cake. Both contained traces of the Life Spice. After some time, we returned to camp. William carried her part of the way, for she was too weak to make it completely on her own. Once back at camp, William could hardly leave her side, for the men-in-arms brought back all her fear. She had lived with fear too long to trust more than one, and William was that one. We learned that her name was Kendra. We delayed another day to allow her time to regain more strength, for she was in no condition to travel just yet.

"Sir Cedric," Brenton called to me. He was the captain of the knights with us.

"Yes, Sir Brenton."

"Our camp is set again. Is there something I can have the men do to keep them occupied?"

Brenton was a good man to have as captain. The men respected him, and he was an efficient leader.

I thought for a moment. "If any of the men want to hunt, we could use some venison. Just tell them to be back by late afternoon. Otherwise, the day is theirs."

"Yes, sir," Brenton replied as he withdrew.

Talea and I checked on Kendra and found William at her side. She had eaten but still looked weary, even though it was just late morning. William walked the few paces to us.

"I think she needs to rest some… I'll watch over her," he said.

"Has she talked to you at all? Who is she, and where does she come from?" I asked.

William shook his head. "I don't know. She's still too disturbed to say much. She's nearly dead from starvation," he said as he looked her way. She had finished a bit of soup and lay down on a blanket spread on the ground.

"We'll come back later," I said.

Talea and I walked away and left William to his charge. We checked back with Brenton on the activity of the men for the day. When there was nothing left to do, Talea and I stood alone somewhat awkwardly.

"Care to take a ride?" I asked.

She looked at me the same way she always did, as if to question my motives. "I suppose so."

We mounted and took a casual ride around Lake Pensing. The lake was large with many vantage points of great beauty. Our horses walked side by side.

"I feel compelled to tell you how important your father has been to me," I said after we had ridden in silence for some time.

She smiled. "I wish I had known him while I growing up."

"He mentored me and prepared my heart for the words of the Prince. He is a noble man, Talea," I said. "When I was a child, he was like a grandfather to me. His heart is kind and so full of zeal for the King."

"Mother talked of him every day," she said. "It was hard to know that we were separated by the Great Sea and that I couldn't see him. Yutan did a great deal for me though…much as a father would do."

I stopped our horses and looked at Talea.

"What is it?" she asked.

"I just realized that you are quite a few years older than me," I commented with a half smile on my face.

"The concept of age is foreign to me," she said. "I have lived my whole life where age is irrelevant. So if you are trying to insult me, you are wasting your time."

I chuckled. "Talea, I'm teasing you."

"Oh?" She looked quizzically at me.

We resumed our ride. I was curious as to how she seemed to see right through people yet couldn't tell when I was teasing.

"Talea, how did you know we were being watched by Kendra when we were at the lake?" I asked.

"I don't know," she said. "I suppose it is something I learned from the Silent Warriors."

"You have helped me a great deal as ambassador already. I cannot read people as you do… Thank you."

She looked over at me. "Are you teasing me again?"

"No, of course not." I was becoming aware of an interesting limitation in Talea's abilities. "How is it that you can't read *me*?"

She immediately turned away and did not answer for some time. "I don't know…" she whispered.

No wonder she continually questions my motives, I thought. For some reason I was as much of an enigma to her as she was to me. I found some comfort in knowing that I was not an open book to her like most people seemed to be.

The rest of our ride was pleasant and filled with talk of the mission that lay ahead. That evening we joined William and Kendra around a small fire. She looked somewhat renewed and even smiled slightly when we approached.

"How are you feeling?" I asked.

"Much better, thank you," she replied politely.

Kendra cradled a cup of hot soup in her hands as she sipped the broth. I wondered what her story was but wasn't sure I should ask. Talea and I sat down on a nearby log.

"Have you lived here your whole life?" I began with a non-intrusive question.

She looked at me and then to the ground. "No, just a few years actually…just since the scynths came."

Talea and I looked at each other as we remembered our encounter with a scynth onboard our ship years ago.

"Scynths?" William asked.

Kendra took a deep breath. "Yes, after my brother and little sister disappeared, things changed quickly. We lived in Elttaes. My father was not wealthy, but we had a comfortable life. One day, my brother came home excited about a story he'd heard about evil knights and a good Prince coming back to life after He'd died in Chessington. My parents and I considered it silly fantasy, but my little sister was taken with it. There was talk of some Code and a Dark Knight… It all seemed too strange and unbelievable. My brother began to tell others and tried to live by this Code. I saw him change, but I still didn't believe his strange stories, and neither did my parents.

"Before long, our city was split between those who believed, like my brother, and those who didn't. Then, when Alexander Histen came to power, everything changed. He sent horrible men to rule our city. The new prefect of Elttaes prohibited the telling of the story and began to imprison those who talked of it. In fact, my brother was in prison the day I woke up and couldn't find my little sister anywhere."

Kendra paused and looked very sad. "That was the day Elttaes was devoured by evil."

I felt a chill creep up my spine.

Kendra continued. "We searched everywhere but soon realized that many people were missing, not just my sister. Father went to the prisons, but many of the prisoners, including my brother, were gone too."

I knew she was talking about the night of our silent exodus from Arrethtrae. It must have been eerie for those left behind, but hearing Kendra describe it firsthand was dramatic. William, Talea, and I were all captivated by her story. She held her cup of soup tightly, but I think she forgot it was in her hands as she recalled this story from her past and gazed at nothing.

"We thought that somehow Histen had taken all of them and killed them," she said. "Then later that day *they* came."

"Who came?" William said gently.

"Those hideous creatures…the scynths!" she said, seeming stunned that we didn't know exactly what she was talking about.

William looked thoroughly confused but waited patiently for the rest of the story. Although I had some vague idea of what a scynth was, I hadn't heard of their presence in Arrethtrae. Talea listened and seemed to understand a bit more.

Kendra shuddered as she remembered the horror. "They flew in like a swarm of insects, but they were much worse. They were like…like scorpions with wings, only much larger."

William's perplexed look told me he was questioning Kendra's sanity.

"Talea and I saw one too, William," I said to confirm her story. "Although it was somewhat dark, and I didn't get a good look at it."

"How could you have been spared the horror of the scynths?" Kendra looked at William. "We heard that all of Arrethtrae was infested with them."

"Please, finish your story, and then we will tell you ours," I said. "What does a scynth look like?"

She paused, as if hoping she couldn't remember. "Like a

monster from a dark nightmare…a hideous creature. Its skin is dark red and leathery. Some are nearly as big as a dog. Its head is small, with razor-sharp teeth and ugly black eyes."

"Something like a bat?" Talea offered.

"Yes! Like a bat, only much larger, and it had a tail that—"

"Stings!" Talea and Kendra said simultaneously.

Kendra looked at Talea. "You know of them then?"

"Yes, I know of them," Talea said.

"My father was stung by one, and he suffered from the pain for many days," Kendra said. "He nearly went mad, but he did not die. Thousands were stung. It was horrible. The strange thing is that Histen's men did not seem to be concerned. None of them were stung. They claimed that the scynths were here because the King had sent them, but I believed otherwise.

"The scynths eventually went away and Father recovered, but life was still awful. People were beaten, daughters were taken, and many were killed. Those evil men made everyone swear allegiance to Histen, but even so, they pillaged every home."

Kendra's eyes began to well with tears, and I felt bad that she was reliving this nightmare to satisfy our curiosity.

William put his hand on her shoulder. "Kendra, you do not have to continue," he said softly. "We can talk another time." I could tell that William felt like her protector now, and each sentence of her story was drawing him closer to her.

"No. I want to finish," she said and straightened her shoulders. She looked at William. "But thank you." She smiled at him briefly while wiping away her tears. With each word, she was regaining some of her lost dignity.

"Father knew of this abandoned hut, for he and my brother often used to hunt in these woods. One night we decided to flee the city and hide in the woods. He was concerned that we would not survive under the wicked rule of Histen's men much longer. We lived in the hut for some time, and it was a temporary relief from the daily oppression of the city, but fear of being found never left our minds.

"One day Father went hunting and did not come back. We waited until the next morning, but he still had not returned. Mother and I searched for days, but we could not find him. We did not want to think of what might have happened. Mother grieved for Father daily, and I sensed that her desire to persevere was beginning to waiver. We could not hunt like Father, so we became hungry. We did not dare return to the city…especially without Father to protect us. We gathered what food we could and barely survived day to day. Father had traps that I checked frequently, which helped, but it was not enough. I ventured far from the hut one morning in search of food and—"

Kendra broke down and began to sob quietly. William put his arm around her, and she leaned on his chest.

"I found him. They had tied him to a tree and tortured him. I'm sure they did not find us because he would not tell them…"

She sobbed heavily. Talea walked over to Kendra and knelt before her. She gently took the forgotten cup of cold soup from Kendra's hands and put her hands on Kendra's.

"I'm sorry," was all she said, but it was enough to comfort Kendra.

"I never told Mother…I couldn't. After many months, she fell sick and died too. I was so lonely. Every day hurt to live."

The evil of Sedah had indeed come to Arrethtrae when the Knights of the Prince left. Here was one story of one family… How many more stories of woe there must have been. *If only you had believed*, I thought. *If only you had believed.*

Although she was a broken woman, Kendra seemed comforted by William's strong arm and Talea's sympathetic eyes.

We left for Elttaes the next morning. I figured we would make it by mid to late afternoon. We did not have an extra horse for Kendra, so she rode with William. The scenery was beautiful and lush. At times we traveled in meadows between the breaks in the thick forest walls. The road was narrow, but it sufficed. After a few hours of riding, we came to a small clearing that ended in a growth of thick trees. The road was the only place where the trees broke open. As we approached, Talea became anxious.

I stopped the men. "What is it, Talea?" I asked.

Her face was stern and a bit fearful. We all listened for a moment, and then Talea quickly drew her sword from her scabbard. A moment later all of our swords were drawn.

"Where, Talea?" I said, feeling the tension of the moment rise.

"All around, Cedric," she said. "All around!"

Kendra held tightly to William's waist, and the stark fear we had seen in her earlier returned.

"Brenton, fall back!" I called to the captain, but it was too late.

They came at us from all sides, and we had no time to form battle lines. In an instant, we were fighting for our lives against a force of renegade warriors that was twice as many as our own. The clashing of our swords filled the forest with the sounds of a desperate battle. This time, there were no Silent Warriors to call... *We* were the warriors. William's fight was most difficult since he had to protect Kendra. I tried to cover his back, but there were vicious men all over. Talea fought like a true Knight of the Prince—as did all of the men. Our enemies were visibly surprised at how skilled our forces were, but we would soon be overrun simply because of their numbers. Three of my men were already down. As we fought, I spotted their leader circling the battle from behind.

"Brenton!" I commanded. "Take two men and make a break for Elttaes!" I shouted above the yells and crashing steel. Elttaes was not too far for a horse at full gallop. This battle would not last long, but at least there was a chance.

"No need, sir. Look!" He pointed to the line of trees.

From the road in the trees to Elttaes came the delicious sight of our rescue. Cullen broke through first, followed by fifteen knights with swords drawn and ready for battle.

Although we were still outnumbered, the fight quickly turned in our favor. Soon there were fewer of them than us. The skill of the Knights of the Prince far surpassed that of any band of renegades. They fell into retreat, but we pursued. It was not enough just to survive—we owed the people of

the kingdom freedom from the likes of men such as these. William, Talea, and a few men stayed behind to care for our wounded.

"Cullen," I called and pointed toward the enemy leader as he entered the trees. He nodded, and we focused our attention on him. After a feverish chase through the trees, we surrounded the man and ordered him to disarm and dismount. I commanded the man to be bound and began questioning him.

"Who are you?" I asked. The man's only reply was a disdainful look and silence.

"Why do you fight against the Prince and His knights?" I was angry, for some of my men were wounded if not dead because of him. At the mention of the Prince, the man spit at me and cursed.

"Your Prince claims to bring freedom to Arrethtrae, but it is not freedom for everyone…only for *His* people!" he replied.

I restrained myself. "The Prince wants the best for all. Only those who work evil deeds are imprisoned and punished."

"Then you admit that there is not freedom for everyone?"

I shook my head. "The freedom you talk of would deny others their freedom. That is anarchy and brings destruction to the kingdom," I replied, trying to quell the anger that was rising within me.

"There is no difference, for the Prince imprisons those who refuse His rule…and there are many!" The man glared at me with hatred in his eyes. "I want the freedom Histen offered."

"The freedom you talk of is self-serving and brings destruction and devastation to those who are not powerful enough to defend themselves. The freedom of the Prince is selfless and brings goodness to everyone…no matter how weak or poor they might be. Only those who are wicked of heart will stand against the Prince, because they are full of pride, arrogance, and selfishness. You and those like you would not hesitate to harm and even kill others to get what you want." My anger became evident in my voice as I leaned closer to this rebellious man's face. "What you do not understand is that someone will always be more powerful than you, and one day he will destroy you to get what he wants. Your freedom is not freedom at all—it is bondage! Those who support Histen are fools who cannot see beyond their own petty lusts!"

I backed away, looked at the man, and let my anger subside.

He did not speak, but I could see the loathing in his eyes. I gazed upon him in pity and bewilderment—how could a heart be so cold and deny things so good? His twisted and despising frown was broken only by a repetition of foolish words full of cursing. I questioned him further to attempt to discover the whereabouts of his men, but he was insolent and made it very clear that he would not cooperate.

"You will be taken to Chessington, where you will stand before the Prince to be judged according to your deeds," I ordered.

The encounter with this man troubled my spirit, for only now was I beginning to understand the depth of wickedness a man's heart could attain. Even under the blessing of a just and noble King, where peace was promised and good health was available for all, where the spirit of brotherhood was desired and prosperity thrived, some hearts refused to yield the evil they clutched so tightly. This was a sad realization—that even in paradise, serpents lingered.

On our return back to the clearing, I had an opportunity to thank Cullen. "You saved us, Cullen. How did you know to come?"

"You said you would follow us a day later, but you didn't arrive," he said. "I could only assume that you ran into problems, so we came to offer help."

"We were delayed when we stopped to help a young woman. Your timing was impeccable, sir," I said. "Did Elttaes greet you well?"

"Yes, quite," he said soberly.

"Your family?" I could tell from his tone that his discovery had not been favorable.

"No one is left, Cedric. Histen's devastation was far-reaching," he stated.

I touched his arm. "I'm sorry, Cullen... I truly am sorry. How is Keely doing?"

"She'll be all right—with time."

We arrived back at the clearing with the leader and four other prisoners. I hurried to my fallen men while Cullen and Brenton took care of the prisoners. None of my men were dead, but William and Kendra were attending one who had taken a thrust to his chest. It was serious, but the Life Spice was strong in all of us, and it was working quickly within this man.

William worked to stop the loss of blood. "Kendra, please fetch my water flask on my horse," he said. She quickly walked the few paces to retrieve it.

Cullen walked over to check on the men. "How are they doing?" he asked.

Kendra's back was to us, but I heard her gasp. She dropped the water flask. As she turned around, her face was pale and her mouth had dropped open.

"Cullen!"

Cullen hesitated, and then his eyes became wide with excitement. "Kendra!"

They ran and embraced each other tightly. Both of them began to weep. Our realization of what was happening was slow but no less shocking. Cullen and Kendra were brother and sister! The odds were a million to one against it, but here we were, witnessing the impossible.

"Keely...what about Keely?" Kendra asked frantically.

"She is fine, Kendra. She's in Elttaes. You will see her soon!" Cullen said with a smile as big as I'd ever seen on him.

Kendra told Cullen of the fate of their parents, and it hurt him terribly, but the joy of seeing Kendra alive was great consolation.

We carefully transported our wounded to Elttaes and rested there for a number of days. We welcomed the respite and enjoyed seeing the reunion of Kendra and Keely. For Cullen and his sisters, it was a time of great rejoicing.

CHAPTER TEN

LEINAD AND TESS

After leaving Cameria, Talea and I journeyed from region to region and city to city helping to establish the Prince's selected prefects and governors. Brenton and his twenty-five knights traveled with us, for there was still an occasional skirmish with Histen loyalists.

We arrived in Daydelon many weeks later and enjoyed a time of fellowship and rest with Leinad and Tess. Leinad's duties were especially challenging since Daydelon was one of the largest cities to be governed, and he had the added responsibility of guarding the prisoners from the entire kingdom.

Talea and I ate a wonderful meal at their palace while Brenton and the men benefited from the comforts and amenities such a city had to offer. After the meal, we all took a walk by the river that ran through the midst of the city. It was a favorite place for both Leinad and Tess. We enjoyed sharing the peaceful stroll with them as Leinad took us to the place where a Silent Warrior had visited him when he was a prisoner of Kergon's so many years ago. I enjoyed seeing the place that had only been an image in my mind from Leinad's stories. Talea walked ahead, arm in arm with Leinad, as Tess and I sat upon a bench beneath a shade tree near the river's edge.

"When Talea was a child, she used to beg me to see her father," Tess said as we looked down the walkway toward them. I saw Talea lay her head briefly on Leinad's shoulder.

"Was it hard raising her without him?" I asked

"She was a delightful girl...full of energy," Tess replied. "It was hard being unable to share her with the one I loved. I could see Leinad in her face every time she smiled. It was also hard not knowing what to tell her, for I did not know exactly what the future held."

"You did a wonderful job, Lady Tess," I said. "Talea is a talented and tough lady."

Tess smiled at me. "Perhaps too tough, Cedric?" she asked as she raised her eyebrows. She must have seen my perplexed look.

"I can see that you have feelings for her, Cedric."

I could feel my cheeks color slightly. I considered denying it, but she continued.

"Please be patient with her... The Silent Warriors took Talea under their tutelage—they so enjoyed her zeal for a challenge. Yutan became a father to her when Leinad could not. She learned their ways and, I'm afraid, their ability to fulfill their missions without emotion. They are, shall we say, elusive—wouldn't you agree?"

Elusive...that's Talea, I thought.

"You are part of her mission, Cedric. In order to fulfill her mission, she can't—won't—allow much more than an elusive friendship."

I thought about what she was saying, and it made a lot of sense. It helped me understand Talea so much better. Part of the mystery of this woman was solved.

I looked at Tess. "Thank you, Lady Tess. I have struggled with understanding Talea since the day I met her, and yet I can't help but be drawn to her. She is a special woman."

"That she is, Cedric. The Prince saw something unique in her from the beginning. That is why she is with you as your assistant. Your mission is vitally important during these formative years of the new kingdom, and He knew your challenges would be many."

"She has been invaluable indeed," I replied. "I am continually amazed at how well she can discern people and even situations, but oddly enough, she doesn't seem to know me at all. Why is that, Lady Tess?"

Tess smiled again and placed her hand on my arm. "That, my dear Cedric, is something you must figure out on your own." She stood up from the bench, and I rose too. "Shall we catch up with them?" Tess motioned toward Leinad and Talea.

Somehow I felt confirmed and better equipped to move forward with the mission the Prince had given me. ◈

CHAPTER ELEVEN

KINGDOM COME

 Over the coming months, the Prince ruled Arrethtrae with wisdom, compassion, and justice. He was not simply a good king—He was a perfect king. Power corrupts even the best of men because of their innate desire to acquire more and more. The Prince, however, was different, for He already owned everything. He wanted the best for His people, not for Himself. Within a few short months, the goodness of His rule had already begun to transform a land and people once ravaged by power-hungry men like Fairos and Kergon, who had ruled regions of the Kingdom as vicious castle lords, and ultimately Lucius himself.

The Silent Warriors all but disappeared, for this was an age of peace and prosperity meant for Arrethtraens. The Silent Warriors' service to the King to protect His people was now accomplished by the Knights of the Prince. Their role of delivering the words of the King to the people was unneeded, for the

King was here in the form of His Son. Their battle against the Shadow Warriors was, for the most part, over, since the Dark Knight and most of the Shadow Warriors were captive in the prison pits of the Wasteland. Many of the Silent Warriors were charged to guard this massive prison. No Arrethtraen knew the whereabouts of the Wasteland, for it was a place of desolation reserved only for Lucius and his evil Shadow Warriors.

The Life Spice thrived in Arrethtrae and soon brought healing and good health to all of the people. It grew everywhere—in the cities, on the hills, and in the valleys. Cities were rebuilt; crops were planted; trade prospered. Roads were built, and places of learning were established to teach many the knowledge of the Prince, which seemed inexhaustible. Every corner of Arrethtrae reaped the benefits of prosperity brought to the land by the Prince's reign. It was a golden era that far surpassed even the glory days of Quinn.

Chessington became the hallmark of greatness in Arrethtrae. It became known as the Beloved City of the King. The palace of the Prince gleamed in its brilliance, testifying to the fact that a grand and noble man reigned over the kingdom. The Prince loved His people, and they loved Him. I remembered that day many years ago, before the great battle, when the Prince had first come to Arrethtrae. I had watched Him care for hungry, dirty children in the streets of Chessington. I would never forget the tears that flowed from His eyes as He felt compassion for the hopeless. I had watched a tear fall from His noble cheek and into the dust of the land. I now knew that He saw the pain of the people and yearned for the future He could bring them.

That tear had watered land that would one day burst forth in abundance under His tender care. This was that day—a day of abundance!

The threat of corrupt deeds by evil men was nearly eliminated. Talea and I traveled without the protection of other knights now, and we could move from region to region much faster. The challenge of our mission to mediate and resolve conflict diminished. We now mostly carried progress reports and news from city to city, as well as mandates from the Prince. I enjoyed most of it, for it was a way to see my friends numerous times throughout the year.

Talea and I became companions in an odd sort of way. With long distances to travel and no one else to talk to, we began to understand each other better…at least as friends. I learned to keep a healthy separation between us emotionally, simply because I knew she wanted it that way. But as hard as I tried, I could not ignore my feelings for her. I kept them closely under guard, however, for I was not sure that she would ever feel the same about me. In fact, I occasionally wondered if she didn't desire our mission to end so she would not have to spend so much time with me. Yet she softened a little over time, and I saw her smile at me more and more. Those were the moments I cherished. Overall I felt awkward—I had never felt this way about a lady before. Unfortunately, I had no one to turn to for guidance. I could not figure Talea out or how I was supposed to feel. This nebulous thing called love seemed so easy for some, but for me it was like trying to sail without the wind.

One aspect of our relationship was not difficult to figure

out however. I came to trust Talea completely. She had Leinad's wisdom and Tess's uncanny discernment…and more. She had learned the ways of the Silent Warriors well and used them to aid me whenever possible. She was invaluable to me as an ambassador in many regions and cities.

The Prince had decreed that a feast was to be held each year in the grand city of Chessington to celebrate the day of victory for the people. Invitations were extended to every man, woman, and child in the kingdom. At the first feast, there was much pomp and ceremony, with delicious cuisine from all across the land. The great Chessington Valley was temporarily transformed into a grand courtyard so that all who wanted to could attend. The feast of celebration lasted five days. At its conclusion, a small goblet of bitter wine was given to all who desired to seal themselves to the King. The Prince stood upon a high platform for all to see.

"People of Arrethtrae!" His noble voice echoed down the valley for all to hear. "You are the heart of the King's kingdom. The depth of Our love for you cannot be measured. We have overcome the Dark Knight, and this is a time to remember Our victory!"

The valley erupted to cheers of adoration. The Prince waited for quiet to return.

"Today we celebrate that victory. The wine in your cup is bitter. Do not drink it if your heart is not completely the King's. To drink unworthily is unforgivable. We drink this bitter wine as a vow to remember

the destruction that living without the Code will bring. It will seal you to the King and to Me forever."

The Prince lifted His chalice high into the air. "One King, one Prince, one Code. The King reigns…and His Son!"

Thousands of voices lifted into the air and repeated the words of the Prince as they drank from their goblets of bitter wine. It was difficult to swallow, for it was indeed bitter. With one swallow, my cheeks became flush and my stomach was upset. The taste lingered long afterward. Some did not drink, for they had come only for the celebration. Without a heart completely sewn into the fabric of the Code, the King, and His Son, there was nothing to compel one to drink the bitter wine.

What a strange way to end the feast, I thought. But who was I to question the Prince?

After the celebration at the Beloved City of the King, each city hosted a celebration feast for those who could not attend at Chessington. The prefects and governors were all given the bitter wine to offer at their feasts as well. Those who drank were sealed to the King and the Prince.

At the third feast, William announced his engagement to Kendra, and I rejoiced with him.

After the fifth feast, Talea was called to embark on ambassador missions on her own. She and I were each assigned assistants. It did not take long for me to grow lonely for her. Even though I had struggled with repressed feelings, in my heart I desired to be near her. However, each year we joined together again to travel to the northern regions of the kingdom just before the yearly feast. Our separation during the year seemed to soften Talea's heart toward me, for which I was thankful, but I expected her to eventually find someone to marry since I did not appear to be the one for her. With each year that passed, I was thankful it never happened. I looked for a wife, but my eyes always came back to Talea. I chose to enjoy my time and my friendship with her—it was the time of year I relished most.

I visited with the Prince whenever I was in Chessington. I always looked forward to meeting with Him because He refreshed my soul like cool mountain water quenches the parched palate of a traveler. After the seventh feast He called for me, and I entered His throne room. I approached and knelt before the King of Arrethtrae.

"Rise up, Cedric… How is my faithful friend?" He asked with a smile on his lips.

I never quite felt comfortable being called a friend of the King, for I knew I did not deserve it. Yet knowing He thought of me as a friend empowered my resolve to not fail Him.

"I am quite well, my Prince," I replied. "Throughout the kingdom, there is peace and prosperity. You have transformed Arrethtrae into a glorious kingdom!"

I lowered my head in deference.

"Your service has been invaluable to me, Cedric. You have done well." He escorted me to the palace garden as we talked. I looked out upon the beautiful city of Chessington as He spoke.

"As an ambassador, you have excelled. How is your performance as a knight?" He asked.

I was taken aback slightly—the years of peace had invited complacency in the honing of certain skills as a knight. There are the skills of a gentleman I was required to rely upon daily as an ambassador, but there are also the skills of a warrior.

"I will not forget Your words, my Lord," I replied. "I will continue my training every day."

"Knighthood is in the heart and in the mind, Cedric," He said.

"Yes, my Lord." I knew that He had once again seen into my heart and now found a lack of vigilance. "I will refocus."

He nodded, and we resumed our walk. This walk, and many others, always seemed to encourage and convict me at the same time. Being with the Prince was like looking into a mirror that reflected the secret truths of my heart—truths that even I did not recognize.

Nine feast celebrations came and went. Each one heralded the incredible blessing of the Prince's rule over Arrethtrae. All manner of sickness was eliminated. The kingdom was young and full of life. I imagined it was like the days of Peyton and Dinan, when the King first established Arrethtrae. The goodness of the Prince seemed to extend to forever. I came to love the annual feast for many reasons. It was an honor to pledge my allegiance to the King and the Prince each year. It was also a time to see all of my friends once again—William, Rob, Barrett, Cullen, Leinad, Tess, and many, many more.

At the conclusion of the ninth feast, the King issued a decree that every Knight of the Prince and every man, woman, and child who was sealed to the King must attend the tenth celebration feast.

Arrethtrae began to resemble the Kingdom Across the Sea—the splendor of the cities, the beauty of the country, and the peace in the hearts of her citizens.

What could ever destroy the greatness of such a land? I wondered.

CHAPTER TWELVE

TALEA!

 It was the tenth year of the reign of the Prince. Talea and I met again in Salisburg to begin our journey northward. It was by far the most difficult trek, for we traveled to the cities beyond the Northern Mountains. Norwex was the largest of the northern cities, and Sir Gunther was both city prefect and regional governor there. Our assistants did not relish the journey, so this year we left them at Salisburg and traveled on our own. The passage to the northern region lay between the Northern Mountains and the Tara Hills Mountain Range.

It was during our visit to a small city named Denshire, between the foothills of these two mountain ranges, that we began to notice a strange thing happening among the people. As we visited with the prefect, Sir Bennington, and many Knights of the Prince, it became evident they felt something was amiss. Talea sensed it too, and I saw a serious look return to her eyes—a look I had not seen for years. Ten years of peace and prosperity would not allow me to imagine anything more serious than disgruntled citizens, but Talea was not convinced.

"Sir Bennington, what is it that seems to be wrong?" We sat side by side at an evening meal that he always hosted for us when we passed through. Two of Bennington's knights had joined us.

He thought for a moment. "I have come to believe that secret meetings are occurring, but I cannot verify my suspicions."

"What do you think these meetings concern?" Talea asked.

"I don't know, Lady Talea," he said. "I've asked the knights to keep a keen ear open for information, but we have turned up nothing." Bennington threw his hands up and leaned back in his chair. "It may be nothing at all, but I am not the only one who has noticed it. It is almost as if the people are…discontent and annoyed."

"Discontent and annoyed?" I asked. "With what?"

"Many have not sworn complete allegiance to the King and the Prince, you know," he replied. "More than half the city will not drink the bitter wine at the celebration feasts and be sealed to the King."

"I understand that, Sir Bennington, but even so they are enjoying the benefits of our benevolent King, are they not? They are not limited, nor is their freedom restricted, as long as they do not harm another or violate the Code. They can travel freely, run businesses, build, discover… What is left?"

The room fell silent.

"To defy," replied one of the knights who had remained silent throughout the meal.

We all looked at him, and I suddenly remembered that the free will of man is like a coin with two sides. The decision to choose good and evil is available to every man. It was a sober realization.

I thanked Sir Bennington for sharing his concern and promised to stay vigilant as Talea and I continued our journey. He redirected the conversation to something uplifting before the evening's end and told us of a spectacular view partway up the mountain range that was well worth the ride if we had a mind to see it.

The following day, Talea and I bid farewell to Sir Bennington and left for the northern cities, but we decided to first climb Crestview Ridge and enjoy the view Bennington had described. It was truly spectacular—almost as though the entire kingdom were before us. We left the ridge and traveled down the northern face of the range and came across a fresh campsite that seemed to disturb Talea.

"What is it, Talea?" I asked.

She looked at me and then to the trees. The air was cool this high up, and I could see her frosty breath as she exhaled. The rose of her cheeks captured my attention. She was beautiful. I had conditioned myself to ignore this part of my life, but now I briefly dreamed of a different path for us. I loved her company, but our mission seemed to prohibit anything more than business. I wondered if there was some other way for us to live. The last two years had been especially difficult. Even though our friendship was deeper, I was not content with it as it was.

"I don't know, Cedric… Maybe it's nothing," she said. "But I have not felt such uneasiness for many years. Something is just not right."

We searched the area for some clue as to who might have camped here. There were numerous fire pits, and I discovered many footprints—all large. A chilling thought swallowed my mind, and I looked over at Talea. She was thinking it too. I knelt down and traced one footprint with my finger. A sickening feeling enveloped my stomach.

"It's time to leave, Talea," I said.

She did not hesitate. We mounted our horses and traveled in silence for some time.

"Have you kept up with your sword training?" she finally asked.

"Nearly every day…my sword and the skills the Prince taught me are my love. It has been difficult at times to find someone to train with, but an imaginary foe is often more cunning than a real one. How about you?"

She smiled at me. "Want to find out?"

"I'll take that as a challenge," I said and returned her smile. "Just remember what happened the last time you challenged me."

She raised one eyebrow, and her smile dissolved into a look of determination. We found a clearing at the base of the mountain where a stream wound its way through the forest trees to eventually spill over a rocky ledge into a waterfall-filled pool.

We dismounted and let our horses graze a few paces away. Talea faced me and drew her sword. I drew mine and bowed respectfully. She did likewise, and we took our stances. I realized that I had never trained with Talea. This would be significantly different than the Intrepid Course. I wondered how difficult this challenge would be.

She advanced with a quick combination. I defended and returned with one of my own. She quickly caught each of my cuts perfectly with the flat of her sword to preserve the edge of the blade. Within moments, our swords collided in a relentless volley of cuts and slices. She thrust; I parried. As the bout progressed, she became more and more aggressive, and I could not resist the urge to do the same. Soon we were in a full-fledged sword fight with neither of us holding anything back. It teetered on the edge of dangerous, but the competitive nature of Talea was enthralling. Her countenance was serious and focused. I found it necessary to tap into every ounce of my skill and ability to keep the fight equal.

We continued long after a reasonable amount of time for training, for neither of us appeared able to relinquish the fight. Not since my training with the Prince had I been so completely challenged. I was thoroughly impressed and found incredible comfort in the knowledge that I could trust Talea's skill with the sword if ever our lives were at stake. The forest faded into the background as I found it necessary to focus exclusively on Talea's moves. We rotated, sliced, cut, thrust, advanced, and retreated in an intense fight. At one point Talea brought a bar-rage of four combinations that put me in steady retreat.

She must be tiring. When the motion of her last cut expires, I will press hard and finish this, I thought.

But I did not see the dip in the ground behind me. As I stepped back, I lost my balance and fell backward. She brought a vertical cut down on me, and I just barely stopped it above my head. I quickly rolled to my feet next to a large fallen tree trunk. She brought another cut down upon me, and I stepped aside, narrowly avoiding her blade. The sword embedded itself into the tree just to the left of me, and she was left trying to withdraw it. I was positioned between her and the tree trunk—too close to execute any moves. She brought both hands to bear on the stubborn sword, but it would not budge. I considered sidestepping to gain room for a slice, but instead I wrapped my left arm around both of hers and held them tightly. Her face was close to mine, and I saw beads of sweat on her brow, cheeks, and upper lip. Both of us were breathing hard. I looked into her dark, captivating eyes, which were full of ferocity. She struggled, then paused and looked into my eyes. I flipped my sword into the air, grabbed it by the steel of the blade, and offered the hilt to her.

"I yield, Lady Talea," I said between breaths.

Her eyes softened, and for a moment a look of genuine admiration crossed her face. I saw in her eyes what I remem-bered catching a glimpse of the first time we met. She released the grip on her sword, and I let loose of her arms. She took my sword without turning her eyes away from mine.

"I accept, Sir Cedric of Chessington," she replied.

I smiled, and we both moved apart slightly. "Thank you for one of the most invigorating challenges with the sword I have ever had. You are a worthy opponent with whom I am honored to serve."

"As are you, Cedric."

Talea and I retrieved her sword and refreshed ourselves with the cold mountain-stream water before resuming our trek. We visited two smaller cities before arriving in Norwex. Sir Gunther welcomed us, and we were soon sitting in his manor around a large wooden table with delicious delicacies before us. I was thankful for the days of travel between visits, or I might have taken on the look of a pregnant horse with all the wonderful meals the prefects offered. His wife and two children joined us for the meal.

"It is good to see you, Lady Talea and Sir Cedric. We look forward to your visit each year. Will you be at the feast coming shortly?" he asked.

"Certainly, Sir Gunther—and you?" I asked.

"We would not think to miss it," he said with a large grin.

Talea sat beside me. I glanced her way and noticed that she was looking at Sir Gunther's adolescent son, whose head was lowered, a smirk on his face.

Sir Gunther was a jolly fellow with a barrel chest to match. His wife was plain but full of life. Their daughter, Ava, was ten and quite shy. Delton was seventeen. Each year he seemed to grow colder toward me, but I attributed it to the struggle of adolescence.

"Your children have grown so much this last year, Sir Gunther." I turned my head. "How have you been, Delton?"

He tried to mask his disdain. "All right…I guess," he replied and then occupied himself with the food on his plate.

"And how are you, Ava?" I asked the young lass.

She smiled and blushed. "I am fine, sir. Thank you."

"The meal was delicious, Lady Raleb," Talea said to Gunther's wife.

"Yes," I agreed. "Thank you very much."

The meal was indeed excellent, and I ate until I was uncomfortable. Afterward, Delton quickly disappeared with one of his friends, and Ava found a doll to play with. Soon only Gunther, Talea, and I were at the table.

"Gunther"—I paused—"have you noticed anything unusual in your city or in the region lately?"

"Why do you ask? Should I have?"

"Sir Bennington of Denshire conveyed some concern about his people, and I was wondering if you'd noticed it as well?"

"Ah…Ben is paranoid, Cedric," he said with a laugh. "All is well in the north. There is an occasional ruckus with the youngsters now and then, but nothing to be alarmed about."

"How about the other city leaders—any problems there?" Talea asked.

"Jaret and Treven have *always* been a problem, but it is nothing out of the ordinary," he said a little more seriously. "Listen, if anything strange is going on, I will certainly let you know. Fair enough?"

"Fair enough," I responded.

That night my sleep was fitful. I was awakened in my bed-chamber by Talea.

"Wake up, Cedric!"

"What is it?" It did not take me long to become alert, for my sleep had not been deep. She lit a candle as I sat up in bed. I noticed that she was fully dressed and ready for the day…including her sword.

She sat on the bed next to me. "Did you notice Delton at supper tonight?"

"Yes, but he…"

"I watched, and he left the manor just a short time ago," she said, looking concerned.

"In the middle of the night?" I asked.

"Yes, in the middle of the night. I think something serious is stirring within him," she said, visibly alarmed.

"Listen, Talea, you missed normal adolescence. I knew of many boys who did the same thing. It was never for any good, you can be assured, but I can only remember one time when they tried to overthrow the kingdom." I said, teasing her.

She looked at me again.

"You never know when I'm teasing you, do you?" I asked, amazed. "You are so discerning… How is it that you cannot read me?"

Her shoulders drooped slightly, and she looked away.

"Are there others you cannot read?" I asked.

"You are the only one." Then she returned to the subject. "Gunther suspects something, but he doesn't know how to describe it, so he denies it. Lady Raleb adores Gunther, dotes on Ava, and wants to redecorate their manor. She has given up on Delton. Ava blushes when you talk to her because she thinks you're handsome. Delton is rebelling against his parents and…"

"And what?" I pressed.

"…and he is involved in something very dark—adolescence or no adolescence." She stood and walked to the open window of my chamber. Then she turned and faced me.

"And I can't read you because—"

Talea's words were cut short by a brief whoosh of air. Her eyes opened wide with a look of horror, and then she fell to her knees. I burst out of bed and grabbed her. Only then did I feel the deadly arrow protruding from her back.

CHAPTER THIRTEEN

A REBELLION BORN

 "Talea!" I screamed as she collapsed in my arms. I yelled for Gunther. My hand quickly turned red from the blood spilling down her back.

"Cedric!" she whispered and grabbed my arm.

"Gunther!" I screamed again as I gently lay Talea on her side.

"Talea…be strong. I will take care of you…be strong!" I pleaded as all of my long-held feelings for her surfaced.

Gunther burst into the room with a lamp and stood shocked for a moment as his mind adjusted to the truth of this disaster. Lady Raleb entered and screamed.

"Help me!" I exclaimed, which broke them from their paralysis.

Within minutes the manor was full of frenzied activity as we tried to tend to Talea and discover what had happened. Gunther ordered his knights to search the surrounding area. Talea was tough, but the pain must have been excruciating. I removed the arrow, and she fell into unconsciousness. The wound was deep, and I was worried. I applied a generous amount of the Life Spice salve to her injury before bandaging it. The blood quickly soaked through.

Please don't die, Talea...please!

I was torn between staying with Talea and searching for the wretch that had done this. Suddenly it dawned on me that the arrow had been meant for me, not Talea.

Lady Raleb left the room and returned with a sickened look on her face, leading Sir Dalphry. "Gunther—Delton is gone!"

Gunther's face turned red with rage.

"Where would he go?" I asked sternly.

"I don't know, Cedric, but I can't believe he would have anything to do with this!"

"What about his friends. Would they know?" I asked.

"Possibly. Sir Dalphry, bring the boy Carlyle here immediately," Gunther ordered.

"Yes, sir."

I continued to apply bandages to Talea's wound until the blood quit soaking through. She moaned and looked pale.

There was more activity in the foyer of the manor. Gunther went to see to it. I briefly left Talea under the care of Lady Raleb so I could hear the end of Gunther's conversation with one of the knights.

"...I don't know how he escaped, but two of the guards are dead!" the knight exclaimed.

I joined them, and Gunther looked angry and embarrassed. "What has happened?" I asked.

"Our prisoner has escaped," reported the knight.

"Prisoner?" I was becoming even more agitated.

Gunther tried to explain. "We arrested a large fellow a few days ago when he was caught stealing from a shop in the city." Gunther's tone was laced with excuse.

"Why didn't you tell me, Sir Gunther?" I asked.

"This fellow has frequented our city many times and never gave us any trouble until now," he explained. "We were going to transport him to Chessington during the next trip, but…"

"What did he look like?" I asked

"Big fellow—he seemed harmless enough, although he had a nasty scar across his left cheek. He was a vagrant. He begged for food usually." Gunther stopped. "This is the first day in nine years that we've had any trouble like this, Cedric. Who would have known?"

I contemplated what I'd heard and was interrupted by the entrance of a young lad and his father. The boy was visibly shaken, almost petrified with fear. Gunther appeared to be feeling the crush of circumstance gone awry.

"Where is Delton, Carlyle?" Gunther asked.

"He…he…is dead." The boy broke down. His words were almost inaudible, but there was no mistake about it.

"What?" Gunther asked, obviously not wanting to believe what he'd just heard. "How?"

The lad was too disturbed to respond quickly enough for Gunther, so he grabbed the boy and shook him. "What happened?"

I pulled Gunther away and sat the boy down on a bench.

"What happened, Carlyle?" I asked as calmly as possible. The boy took a deep breath and exhaled.

"Delton wanted to meet me tonight. He told me he had something important to show me. He said something about Sutak being the 'Keeper of the Map' and that he had to set him free." The boy paused for another breath.

I looked at Gunther. "Sutak?" I asked. Gunther bit his lip and turned away.

"Sutak was the name of the prisoner," replied the knight who had earlier reported him missing.

The boy continued. "Delton stole your key to the prison, Sir Gunther. I was supposed to meet him in an alley by the stables, but when I got there…"

"What? What did you find?" I asked.

"There were six…maybe seven huge men, and Delton was with them. I hid between two buildings because I was scared. They would have killed me too!" he blurted, and tears streamed down his face.

"Delton said that Mr. Jaret would help him." The boy's story was disjointed, but every passing moment painted a picture that reeked of evil.

"Take us there, Carlyle," I said. "There is much at stake."

I ran back to my bedchamber to check on Talea and did not dare tell Lady Raleb the news of her son. I quickly donned my breastplate, sword, and boots. I leaned close to Talea and felt her shallow breath on my cheek. I brushed the hair from her face and kissed her forehead.

"Please take care of her for me, Lady Raleb," I said.

"I will, Cedric."

We followed Carlyle to the alley and found Delton on the ground beside the wall of a brick building. Gunther knelt down and cradled his son in his arms, and tears welled up in his eyes. I held the lamp close to see Delton's wound and saw not only the wound but also the weapon that had made it. Delton's hands were wrapped around the hilt of a long and wicked knife. I opened his fingers and saw what I did not want to see—the mark of the Dark Knight. This was the dagger of a Shadow Warrior. Delton took a shallow breath and coughed—he was still alive!

"Delton!" Gunther exclaimed.

"Father…" Delton's faint speech was barely perceptible.

"Who did this to you?" Gunther asked.

"He said he would make me a great leader…" The boy coughed, and blood trickled down his chin. "I freed Sutak and they…lied…"

"Why did they want Sutak?" I asked.

Delton was fading quickly. "He was…the Keeper of the Map…" His entire body spasmed in pain.

"The map to what, Delton? To what?" I asked.

He gasped for one last breath. "The…Wasteland…" His eyes rolled back in his head, and his body went limp. Gunther held Delton tightly. His large shoulders shook as he was overcome with grief.

All of us froze. We dared not believe what we'd just heard. If these men were indeed Shadow Warriors and they knew the location of the Wasteland, all of Arrethtrae was in jeopardy.

How many Shadow Warriors are loose? I wondered. *How can this be?*

Everyone was too stunned to move, and yet I knew that I must get to Chessington as fast as possible. *Do I dare leave Talea? What if she dies?* I felt plagued by more questions than answers.

I pulled the Shadow Warrior's blade from Delton for proof of this evil plot and stood up.

"I must leave, Gunther. The Prince must know as soon as possible," I said. The urgency of the situation began to build within me, but the sound of many approaching men thwarted my intentions. I drew my sword, as did my fellow knights. Within moments we were surrounded by hundreds of ill-intentioned men.

"Jaret!" exclaimed Gunther. "It had to be you."

The man named Jaret smiled a vengeful smile.

"Why, Jaret? Why are you doing this?" Gunther asked.

"For the same reason men all over the kingdom are doing it, Gunther." He sneered. "Power! We are tired of following the Prince and His ridiculous Code. Histen has promised us power…something we will never have under the Prince."

"And you really believe Histen will honor his promise?" I asked incredulously. "Look what his men have already done to Delton. You will be next!"

Jaret glanced down at Delton. "They killed him because he was the son of Gunther… We have not sworn our allegiance to the King, and we never will."

He pointed at us. "Take them to the prison cells!" Jaret ordered.

CHAPTER FOURTEEN

VENGEANCE
OF A DRAGON

The rebellion began in Norwex, but we had no way of knowing how many other cities had joined or if they even knew of the rebellion. The tenth feast of celebration was just five weeks away. It was to be the greatest of them all, for everyone sealed to the King was to attend.

I felt helpless as I sat on the cold stone floor of the cell. The hours passed. More and more cells were being filled with Knights of the Prince and anyone bold enough to stand against the rebellion. We asked the newest prisoners for news of the city, and it sounded like the rebels were in complete control. I inquired of Talea, but there was no word from anyone. I was nearly out of my mind wondering what had happened to her. I did not know if she was dead or alive.

If the Shadow Warriors were successful in finding the Wasteland and releasing Lucius, I did not dare to think how far the rebellion would run. There was still a chance that the

Silent Warriors would thwart their plan. It was all I could hope for.

Two days passed with no food or water. We were becoming faint and petitioned the rebel guards, but they were completely apathetic toward us. Finally, on the morning of the third day, water and a bit of food was given to us. But the waiting was more agonizing than the painful hunger in my stomach. Our cells were full, and we heard that the rebels had killed many. They had made a temporary prison camp, where many others were evidently taken. Gunther tried to find out about his wife and daughter but was unsuccessful.

The hours passed slowly, and the days even more slowly. Three weeks passed, and I began to wonder if there was any hope of being discovered by our fellow knights this far north in the kingdom. On the morning of the twenty-second day, our food and water came as usual. Three guards delivered our food. Two entered the prison hallway, but the third was delayed. When he came in, he wore a hood that covered most of his face. He did not stop at the nearest cell, as was usual, and the prisoners there made a ruckus. The other two guards turned around to see what was the matter.

The hooded guard drew a sword that I recognized in an instant. The other guards dropped their trays of bread and began to draw their swords, but Talea was too quick for them. Within a moment, both guards lay dead on the stone floor. We were all stunned to silence, and I couldn't believe my eyes. Talea threw back the hood and searched the cells. All of the knights were to their feet and quietly cheered. I was ecstatic to see that pretty face of hers and called to her quietly. Talea found me, opened my cell, and gave the keys to the other knights within, who in turn quickly opened all the other cells. I grabbed Talea and smiled with a joy that I had thought was lost forever. I hugged her tightly.

"Ah…careful," she said and winced.

"I'm sorry…" I felt foolish for momentarily forgetting her wound. "Thank the King you're alive!" I stepped back and looked at her. "How?"

"I'll explain later," she said and smiled at me as she never had before. She briefly put her hand on my cheek. For almost ten years I had looked for the smallest hint of affirmation from Talea, and I found it in that single small act.

"I brought you a present," she said and opened her cloak to reveal my sword. She handed it to me, and I numbly took it as I tried to shake myself back to the reality of our situation. She turned to exit the cell, but I grabbed her arm. She looked back at me over her shoulder.

"Thank you!" I was grateful for more than my sword.

She smiled a knowing smile.

We quickly and quietly marshaled ourselves in the prison hall. Gunther, Talea, and I moved closest to the door that exited the hall.

"There are five guards in the main guardroom… Two are still asleep," Talea whispered to the men. Approximately forty Knights of the Prince stood behind us, waiting to fight for the King—bare-handed if need be.

Gunther spoke softly. "There are three other prison halls

like this one…all probably full of fellow knights. It's a good bet they are being given their rations now too. We must move quickly to catch them off guard."

"Split into three teams—one for each hall," I ordered. "Secure the doors until we can recover the main guardroom and get swords to you."

We readied ourselves and opened the door slowly until the room was visible. The first guard spotted us, and we burst into the room—all forty of us. Talea and I made quick work of the nearest two guards. Gunther and a fellow knight recovered their swords and joined us as we engaged the remaining guards. Within moments, we controlled the main guardroom. Shortly after that we controlled the entire prison. We locked the rebel guards in the cells and formulated a plan to recover the city.

We exited the prison and discovered no resistance in the city of Norwex. It was baffling—there appeared to be no rebels anywhere other than the prison. We encountered women, children, and an occasional older man, but no rebels. At the location of the temporary prison, we found only a handful of guards, and they relinquished without a fight. We released all of the prisoners. Two Knights of the Prince were among them, as well as Gunther's entire household.

"Gunther!" Raleb shouted and ran to him with little Ava following close behind.

"Raleb! You are all right!"

Gunther knelt down and hugged Ava tightly.

Talea walked to Raleb and embraced her. "Thank you."

"I am so thankful you survived, Lady Talea," Raleb said.

Talea turned to me. "When the rebels came to the manor, Lady Raleb hid me in a secret chamber with food and water. The Life Spice healed me, but I did not dare leave until I felt I could use my sword effectively. It was difficult to be patient."

I turned to the two knights that had been held captive in the temporary prison, hoping they may have seen something to help explain what had happened.

"Gentlemen, can you shed some light on what has happened?" I asked.

"Yes, Sir Cedric…" one said, then paused as if unwilling to reveal what he knew. "They came from the northeast. Shadow Warriors…thousands of them!"

His words hit me like a hammer. "Lucius? Did you see…Lucius?"

The knights lowered their eyes and nodded affirmation.

So the pits of the Wasteland gave up their evil host, I thought. *Simply because the wicked heart of man wanted it.*

"And the rebels?" Gunther asked.

"They joined the Shadow Warriors and left Norwex over seven days ago. We don't know where they were going," replied one of the guards.

"I know!" I turned to face Gunther. "The tenth feast is less than two weeks away. It is a gathering of all the Knights of the Prince and all people sealed to the King. Lucius's escape, this rebellion, and the tenth feast are no coincidence. All cities will be vulnerable if the Knights of the Prince are all at Chessington. The Shadow Warriors are probably leading rebellions throughout the kingdom."

The realization that the entire kingdom was in jeopardy slowly dawned on us all.

Talea broke in. "A gathering of all of the King's people in one valley, completely unaware that Lucius is leading a king-domwide rebellion to destroy them…"

How quickly paradise could be lost again because of the pride and greed of evil men! I knew that Lucius's vengeance would be satisfied by nothing less than the death of the Prince and of all His people.

"Gunther, you must gather all people sealed to the King and get them to Chessington," I said. "Avoid all cities. Use the Knights of the Prince for protection. It will become more dangerous the closer you get to Chessington, so be extremely careful. Talea and I must ride ahead and try to get to the Prince before the feast and warn Him. It may be too late already—Chessington is a distant ride from here."

Gunther nodded. "I understand, Sir Cedric. The King reigns…"

"And His Son!" I replied.

Talea and I quickly gathered provisions, rounded up fresh horses, and rode south to the Beloved City of the King. How we would make it through the forces of Lucius and the rebels was something I dared not contemplate. I just knew we had to do it, for we were the only ones aware of the impending destruction! 🔲

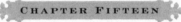

CHAPTER FIFTEEN

FROM THE CAVERNS OF SEDAH

 Talea and I rode as hard as our horses would allow. I was thankful for a half moon, which enabled us to ride even at night. We slept three to four hours a day and traveled the rest. By the fifth day, we and our steeds were spent, so we camped in a wooded area just north of Salisburg for an entire night to recover and build our strength. From Salisburg on, we knew it would be difficult to avoid Shadow Warriors and rebels. All of the Knights of the Prince and those sealed to the King would have already left their cities many days ago to make the tenth feast. Talea and I would find no help from anyone… We were alone in enemy territory.

We built a fire for warmth that night but kept it small. Although I was exhausted, my apprehension kept me from any sleep that was refreshing. I wanted to go on but could not. It was like trying to run in the knee-high waters of a sandy shore. I rolled over on my blanket and saw the peaceful face of Talea sleeping next to me. The chirping of the crickets and the cool night air were familiar and soothing but not as comforting as seeing Talea near me. My thoughts turned to her. Only when I thought I might lose her had I realized just how much she meant to me.

"The one thing I have desired to win the most I have failed in, my sweet Talea…your heart," I whispered softly.

Talea slowly opened her eyes, and I became embarrassed. I hadn't realized she was still awake. She looked at me and did not hide her heart from her eyes this time. The flames of the fire radiated a soft glow that reflected from her cheeks. I fumbled for an excuse, but she put her fingers to my lips.

"You won my heart the day we met, Cedric, but I was incapable of letting you know. These years away from you helped me overcome that."

For a moment I thought I was hearing the wishful words of my own dream, but the touch of her fingers on my lips was too real to be the wisps of a dreamscape. I reached for her hand to affirm what she said, and she took my hand in hers. The warmth of my cheeks subsided, and I gently kissed her hand.

"Tomorrow the kingdom may fall, but tonight I have found contentment in the welcome of your words," I said quietly.

She smiled and closed her eyes once again. "That is why I could never read you, Cedric," she whispered. "My feelings for you clouded my discernment."

The mystery of the fair maiden is solved, I thought to myself, delighted. "Sleep well, Lady Talea."

"And you, Sir Cedric."

Maybe my sleep would be peaceful after all.

I awoke in the early morning to the nervous neighing of our horses a short distance away. I opened my eyes but did not move, for I was immediately aware of a dark presence. I could hear an occasional flutter of wings that sent chills down my back. Talea was asleep, and her hand was still in mine. I scanned as much of the area as possible, moving only my eyes, but I could not see anything. Tremendous fear began to well up within me. I slowly raised myself on my left arm to look over Talea and saw the monsters of a nightmare surrounding us—scynths! One large scynth was just an arm's length away from Talea's back. I could see two more in the trees behind it.

While keeping a close eye on the scynth behind Talea, I slowly squeezed her hand, hoping she would not move too abruptly. I did not dare look over my own back. Talea moaned slightly, and the scynth behind her spread its wings and raised its deadly tail high into the air. I could see the finger-long stinger protruding from its tail. It looked as sharp as a viper's fang, and a drop of poison glistened on its tip. Talea opened her eyes and immediately registered the fear on my face.

"Shh," I said quietly.

The scynth opened its mouth to reveal dozens of razor-sharp teeth. Black eyes glared at me, dark as the depths of the caverns of Sedah. It began to hiss and looked as though it was ready to strike at any moment. It was a hideous creature that seemed to live for the sole purpose of striking fear into the hearts of men.

Talea searched my eyes for help, but I was at a loss for what to do. I released her hand, and she carefully placed her knife in mine. Just as my hand encircled the grip of the knife, the scynth jumped into the air. Its wings flapped, and the tail whipped from its high position to beneath its body toward the exposed back of Talea. I lunged across her and plunged the knife down onto the striking tail, hoping I would not miss. The knife found its mark as it penetrated clear through the tail and embedded into the ground. The fanglike stinger stopped

just short of Talea's back. The scynth screeched in pain and flapped its wings violently, trying to free its tail. Talea reached for her sword, but she was momentarily trapped beneath me as I held the knife firmly to the ground. The scynth dropped to the ground and lashed at my hand with its wicked teeth. I released the knife and withdrew my hand just before its jaws clamped down on the handle of the knife.

I grabbed Talea's shoulder, and we rolled away from the enraged creature. I became aware of the screeches and flutters of other scynths and wondered how long before they, too, attacked. With swords drawn, we rose to our feet just in time to see another scynth screaming toward me with its tail striking forward beneath it. I ducked and felt the whoosh of air on my neck as the poisonous stinger whipped past my head. Talea executed a powerful slice above me and nearly cut the creature in two. I recovered, and we guarded each other's back. The other scynths remained in the trees—staring and hissing. My heart was pounding, and my legs hurt from the sudden exertion of the encounter. The creature on the ground flailed and screeched violently as it tried to free itself from the knife through its tail. We slowly moved toward our horses a short distance away. Once clear of the camp and the scynths, we quickly mounted our steeds and hastily left the area. A few moments later we stopped and looked back to the trees.

Talea looked shaken. "Are you all right?" I asked.

"I will be," she replied. She shook her head. "That was absolutely horrible. It can only mean one thing, Cedric."

I turned and looked to the south. "Yes…I know."

Talea reached for my hand. "Thank you!"

"You're welcome and thank *you*!" We both took a deep breath. "If you'd like, we can go back for your knife," I said with a smile.

She laughed. "I think I'd rather leave it with the scynth."

Talea and I rode a bit farther and then stopped briefly for a quick breakfast before continuing our journey south. Three days later, on the morning of the second day of the tenth feast, we approached the Chessington Valley. On any normal day, we could've made Chessington by noon, but this was not a normal day. We crested a ridge of the rolling green plains north of the valley and nearly froze at what we saw. A massive army of destruction larger than any force I had ever seen blanketed the area. We quickly retreated and found better cover in a grove of trees, which also afforded a higher and clearer vantage point to spy on the force. We moved to the edge of the trees, and as we watched, smaller armies continued to join from all directions except the south, where Chessington was ironically celebrating the tenth year of peace and prosperity of the kingdom.

"Talea, even if all of the King's Silent Warriors were here, we still could not overcome an evil army of this size. Look, even more are still coming!" I exclaimed. "What could Lucius have promised the cities of the kingdom to raise such an army as this?"

Talea shook her head in disbelief. "How can we possibly get through this mass of warriors to the valley?" she asked.

"You can't!" The voice came from the trees behind us. Talea and I quickly turned about, drawing our swords as we did. We were so preoccupied with the evil before us that we hadn't sensed a presence behind us—five massive Shadow Warriors. The appearance of a Shadow Warrior is daunting indeed, but these wore a look of consuming hate and revenge for their years condemned to the prison pits of the Wasteland.

As they glared at us, they immediately recognized the mark of the Prince upon our breastplates and swords. Two of them cursed and charged upon us. The other three followed close behind. Though tired from the long journey, my heart quickened, and the rush of the fight immediately empowered my arms and legs to battle-ready strength. I did not dare consider our odds of surviving. I did, however, momentarily consider the cost of our failure—the kingdom. I tried to formulate some plan that would allow Talea to escape to warn the Prince of the evil army that would soon encompass Chessington. Whatever that plan, it would surely cost me my life.

Talea and I readied ourselves as the first two brutes stormed at us without hesitation. We separated slightly, for this fight would require more from us in the way of speed, power, agility, and strategy than any other fight before.

Talea feigned the look of a frightened, inept knight—at least I hoped it was a ploy. The other Shadow Warrior bore down on me aggressively. We needed to overcome these first two adversaries quickly if there was any chance of surviving.

Talea's foe initially made a massive vertical cut upon her. She used both hands on her sword to stop the blow of his wicked sword, but it appeared to be too much for her to stop. She gave with the blow and dropped to the ground on one knee. The warrior smiled evilly and recoiled for another vertical strike. As he did, Talea spun her body with the speed of a panther and brought her screaming sword around in an arc with such power that her blade brought a quick and immediate end to her shocked opponent. He fell to the ground with a thud.

My adversary recklessly brought blow after blow as I countered and retreated slightly. He thrust at my chest, which I quickly parried left and followed with a thrust of my own. He could not recover quickly enough, and my blade penetrated deep into his torso. He fell to the ground, unable to utter his final curse.

The remaining three warriors appeared momentarily shocked at the sight of their two fallen companions. Two of them engaged me while the other faced Talea. We would have to rely upon all the training of the Prince if we hoped to survive these wicked adversaries. The two I faced immediately separated to divide my attention. I had trained for such situations in the past but never against Shadow Warriors. I quickened the speed of my sword to counter their cuts and tried to maneuver toward a large tree to protect at least one side of me. Talea was heavily engaged with her opponent but was holding her own.

One of my challengers executed a quick combination, which I countered, but the other saw my distraction and lunged with a thrust aimed at my torso. I turned sideways and moved just enough to miss the thrust from behind me. His sword passed close to my chest as the other warrior brought a mid-high cut at me. I jumped toward the warrior with the extended thrust to miss the other's cut, and I heard him grunt as I impacted his chest with the full force of my body, which sent him reeling backward far enough for me to recover and advance on the other warrior. My time was short, so I abandoned caution and attacked so quickly that he did not expect the final vertical cut that nearly caused him to lose his sword. He fumbled for just a moment—a moment too long—and my sword found its mark as he dropped to the ground dead.

I turned to face my remaining foe, only to see his blade racing toward my throat. I pulled my sword up just in time to meet his powerful blow, but it was too much force for me, and my sword was thrown from my grip. I screamed as his blade ripped through my left shoulder. I fell to the ground to retrieve my sword, but the Shadow Warrior swung his deadly weapon high in the air to deal his final deathblow. He did not finish, however, for just as he was about to strike, Talea's blade sliced through his chest from behind. She had been victorious over her enemy and had come to my aid at the last moment.

It was all over very quickly. I leaned up against a tree, and Talea came to attend to my wound. She retrieved a bandage from her horse and wrapped my shoulder speedily since we were not sure if others might come. As she did, I studied the region and realized that we had to travel farther east to skirt the army before resuming our route to the valley. It would cost us time, but we had no choice. I hoped we would reach the valley before Lucius had positioned his forces and begun his attack. Our task seemed futile, for I felt like we were attempting to outrun a Banteen dust storm with no place to hide. At least the Shadow Warriors on the ground about us would not foil our warning to the Prince.

CHAPTER SIXTEEN

THE TENTH FEAST

 By midafternoon Talea and I crested the east ridge of the Chessington Valley just north of the city. The valley pulsed with celebration and ceremony. With the exception of the people from Norwex, all the King's people and all the Knights of the Prince appeared to be present. It was the largest gathering in the history of Arrethtrae—many, many thousands. The sky was bright blue, and the sun radiated its warmth on the King's tenth celebration feast.

We paused for just a moment to look northward toward the looming disaster. Even now I could see the faint lines of Lucius's forces coalescing on the valley. Talea and I pressed our steeds into their final full gallop and reached the edge of the courtyard of the feast. We forced our way through the throng of people to the main platform, where I hoped to find the Prince. A ceremony to honor the Knights of the Prince was in process as we ran to the front of the platform to capture the Prince's attention.

The knights all applauded, perhaps assuming we had been delayed due to some inconvenience. I saw my fellow knights smiling in their ignorance, full of glee. But some saw my bandaged shoulder, and their faces turned serious in an instant.

The Prince held up His hands to hush the knights and the people. His countenance was unexpectedly stern, almost as though He knew my news was of ill report. The throng fell to silence for the Prince.

"Sir Cedric of Chessington, what is so urgent?" He asked.

I shouted loud enough for the knights to hear as well. "My Prince, we have just returned from Norwex. Lucius and the Shadow Warriors have escaped from the Wasteland! All of the cities of the kingdom have rebelled and have joined forces with him. They approach the valley as we speak!"

Exclamations and murmurings rumbled through the mass of people as my words were passed from mouth to mouth. The Knights of the Prince looked shocked and alarmed. Some drew their swords. Leinad, Tess, Gavinaugh, Keanna, Weston, William, Rob, Barrett, and Cullen stepped forward, nearer to the Prince.

In a moment, fear swept through the assembly as everyone began to scan the horizons for this massive force of destruction of which I had just spoken.

The Prince looked to the horizon as well, but I saw no fear upon His noble brow. His eyes could always see what we could not. I studied His face, for in His countenance rested my assurance and my faith in the future. Somehow, the powerful confidence of His kingly form did not falter for even an instant.

How…how, my King, can there be any salvation for Your people now? I thought in wonder as I beheld the glory of His face.

He dropped His gaze to Talea and me. "You have risked your lives to bring Me this warning. Well done, Cedric. Well done, Talea."

The Prince turned to face His knights. "Knights of the Prince, surround My people with your swords drawn and ready for battle. Do not engage the enemy until you hear My command to do so. Go!"

All the knights drew their swords and began to disperse to the perimeter of the people. The Prince called Leinad, Tess, Gavinaugh, Keanna, Weston, William, Rob, Barrett, Cullen, Talea, and me to His side.

"Follow Me," He commanded and marched us through the mass of people to the northern edge of the temporary courtyard.

As we walked, Lucius and the armies of the cities encompassed the Beloved City of the King and the Knights of the Prince, intending to bring battle to the valley once again. Great were the numbers of the evil army that surrounded us—like the sands of the sea. We broke from the northern edge of the courtyard, a fair distance up the valley, as our fellow warriors positioned themselves around the perimeter of thousands of frightened people.

It was a peculiar feeling. Ten years earlier, in the same valley with many of the same warriors, a similar battle had been fought—only *we* had been in the hills with the element of surprise to our advantage. I had hoped it would be the battle to end all battles, but today was proving me wrong.

The Prince and our small band of knights broke from the people and continued twenty paces into the open country of the higher valley—and waited.

"Have faith, My knights," was all that the Prince said. Once again I was in the company of heroes. These men and women were the emblem of the Code the kingdom had lived by for many years. It was an honor to stand with them this hour…even if it would be our last.

We did not have to wait long, for Lucius's confidence in his victory negated any need for a surprise attack. They came from the east, they came from the west, and they came from the north. It looked so hopeless. Not even the Silent Warriors were with us.

Lucius marched south down the valley to meet the Prince. Those who followed him seemed to stretch forever. As he neared our position, he halted his forces some forty paces away. He broke from the mass with five of his Shadow Warriors by his side and approached the Prince. They dismounted and covered the remaining few paces.

Here before us stood the epitome of wickedness. I remembered facing Lucius many years ago in the streets of Chessington just before the Prince called us home. The vengeful wrath that shone upon his face today was more ferocious than ever before. I supposed the years in the pits of the Wasteland had taken the bitter heart of an evil warrior and seared the lust for revenge even deeper into his every fiber. He bore the deep scar of his previous encounter with the Prince…a scar that had never let him forget his failure.

The Prince of all that was good stood face-to-face with the prince of all that was evil.

"You have no escape… Your destruction is in my hand!" Lucius said with vehemence as he clenched his fist to emphasize his words.

"Your arrogance has always been your weakness, Lucius. And it will be your destruction," the Prince replied. His voice was stern but amazingly calm.

This enraged Lucius—he seemed desperate to force the Prince to yield.

Lucius's face crinkled in an expression of hatred. "Bow before me, and I will kill you and only half of these pitiful Followers of yours. If you do not, I will not leave one beating heart in this valley or in all of Chessington!"

"I will not bow before you, nor will you draw one drop of blood from any of My people." The Prince's voice began to rise, and His wrath began to emanate so powerfully from His being that Lucius cowered for a brief instant, and his men stepped back. Even now, with all odds against the Prince, they still feared Him.

"In your contorted mind you believe you are free, Lucius, but you are actually a prisoner of your own future—a future that will end today!" the Prince said fiercely.

Lucius recovered and sneered at the Prince. He spoke loudly for all to hear. "Look to the hills! What I see is *your* destruction—not mine!" he bellowed.

The Prince glared at Lucius with eyes that burned like fire. "Yes, Lucius. Look to the hills—your judgment draws nigh!"

The Prince pointed upward to a ridge just east of Chessington, where Lucius's forces were not. There, upon a gallant white stallion, was the form of a lone Man carrying a longbow and one flaming arrow. He could not be mistaken for any other, for His form was too majestic. It was the King! He rode His steed along the ridge of the valley and into the forces of Lucius. They parted like the wake behind a ship to allow His passage until He sat abreast of our position in the lower valley. I glanced at Lucius—the arrogance and vengeance in his face had turned to consternation.

The King drew back His bow and let fly the single arrow. Every eye in the valley watched the fiery arrow fly toward us. It arced high across the evil army and plunged into the soft soil but a few paces to our right. The flame extinguished immediately. Then very slowly, something strange began to emanate from the head of the embedded arrow. Like the oozing of blood from a wound, a bright, fire-red substance began to spread across the lush ground. It seemed to devour the grass and Life Spice plants—gaining momentum with each passing moment. I saw Tess grab Leinad with a fearful look upon her face.

"Vactors!" she whispered. Leinad looked anxious too.

"What is this?" Lucius exclaimed and looked at the Prince.

"Vactors of Fire, Lucius, and your judgment," He replied.

The Shadow Warriors standing with Lucius stepped backward in sheer panic, away from the spreading fire-red mass.

The Prince turned to us. "Do not fear. You have been

sealed to the King through the bitter wine. Stand still." His calm voice helped, but the panic so evident in Lucius and the Shadow Warriors was unnerving.

Lucius and his men ran toward their horses as the leading edge of the Vactors of Fire reached the feet of the Prince. They did not touch His feet but bypassed and continued to spread at an incredible speed. I reached for Talea's hand as the Vactors of Fire neared us…and passed on. Like a rock thrown in a still lake creates ripples that flow outward, the Vactors of Fire spread outward from the arrow. A pungent orange fog rose up from the consumption of the vegetation. The fire-red color of the Vactors combined with the rising fog gave the impression that fire was burning up the valley.

Lucius was the first to feel the torment of the King's judgment. The Vactors of Fire reached his feet and began to envelop his legs. He screamed and turned to face the Prince one last time. He fell to his knees with a clenched fist in the air and a curse on his lips…and then he was gone!

The Vactors of Fire reached the front edge of Lucius's army and consumed them without a moment of hesitation. Soon the entire army was in complete hysteria, but there was no escape. They had come in rebellion against the Prince and the King. It was hard to watch their demise, but it was their own doing. The Vactors of Fire raced across the valley, consuming everything and everyone in their path—except those who had been sealed to the King by drinking the bitter wine. They spread in all directions to the uttermost parts of the kingdom, and then the episode ended as quickly as it had begun. When all had been consumed, the fire-red color of the Vactors faded to a dull gray, and the pungent orange fog slowly dissipated.

The King rode His steed down the valley to the stunned people below and dismounted near the Prince. The majesty of the King and His Son overwhelmed us. This was the end of one kingdom and the beginning of another. We stood here before Them, saved and alive, simply because They loved us. The entire valley full of people knelt before Them unified in awe and adoration. He was our King... We were His people.

The King placed His hand on His Son's shoulder.

"It's time to take Our people home, Son," He said, with love and admiration in His eyes.

The Prince placed His hand upon the King's.

"Yes, Father... Let Us take them home, where We will live with them forever, and there will be no more sorrow!"

The King lifted His hands to the sky. "Rise up, faithful servants of the King," He exclaimed for all to hear. "Rise up and be glad, for I will take you to a new kingdom!"

Leinad stood, raised his sword high in the air, and shouted. "The King reigns...and His Son!"

The Chessington Valley erupted in unison. "The King reigns...and His Son!"

The people rejoiced, and I embraced all of my fellow brothers and sisters in victory. Lucius and his Shadow Warriors were gone—it was finally over!

I found Talea and pulled her close to me. I kissed her, and she embraced me. Victory was sweet—as was our newfound love for each other.

CHAPTER SEVENTEEN

THE FINAL KINGDOM

 The King and the Prince led us to the waiting armada of ships in the Chessington harbor. The Silent Warriors searched the entire kingdom for any others of those sealed to the King, including the people of Norwex, and brought them to the docks.

We are sailing to a new kingdom, where a New Chessington awaits us. It is our final voyage to the ultimate kingdom. The King promises new life and adventure that we cannot imagine. My life has already been an adventure of wonder, for the King and the Prince brought me from the depths of peasantry to the heights of nobility. Without the Prince, I was empty and without hope, but now I am a fellow heir of the new kingdom. I became a Knight of the Prince because I believed in Him. It is a faith I will never let go of, for His love for me is endless. His love for you is endless too… Do *you* believe?

The King reigns…and His Son!

DISCUSSION QUESTIONS

To further facilitate the understanding of the biblical allegory of this series, a few discussion questions and answers are provided below.

CHAPTER 1

1. The Great Sea represents the separation between heaven and earth. On his voyage to the Kingdom Across the Sea, Cedric meets Cullen of the United Cities of Cameria. What does Cameria represent?
2. Cedric explains that Cameria stood strong with Chessington when times became difficult. In what way is this an allegory for today?

CHAPTER 2

1. When Cedric arrives at the Kingdom Across the Sea, he is reunited with his friends. They cannot enter the great city because the Silent Warriors are guarding the entrance. Only the Prince is deemed worthy to enter. Find a passage in Revelation where only Jesus is worthy to accomplish a task.
2. Cedric and the rest of the people could only come to the King by trusting in the Prince. What Bible verse tells us that the only way to the Father is through Jesus?

CHAPTER 3

1. The Prince has prepared a home for each of His Followers. What Bible passage promises a home in heaven for each believer?

2. All of the Followers of the Prince are invited to partake in a grand feast. This is symbolic of a great supper that is to take place in heaven, described in Revelation 19:7–9. Can you find a parable that Jesus taught concerning a great supper?

3. In this chapter, Cedric is surprised to discover that not only is Leinad still alive, but he looks young again. Leinad explains that the Life Spice has restored his body. What does the Life Spice represent here?

CHAPTER 4

1. In this chapter we finally learn the mysterious identity of Talea. Who does she represent?

CHAPTER 5

1. The Prince continues to teach and train the Knights of the Prince. He warns Cedric that "the most dangerous threat of evil is when it seems to be absent." This foreshadows the rebellion yet to come. Why is this statement so true even today? Find Scripture to back up your answers.

2. This chapter tells of Lucius's reign of terror in the kingdom under the pseudonym of Alexander Histen. What time in Bible prophecy does this represent?

3. Read Hosea 6:1–3 and Hosea 14:1–7, and describe how this parallels when Gabrik relays the repentant words of the citizens of Chessington to the King and the Prince.

CHAPTER 6

1. The Prince and His army travel to defend Chessington against Lucius and all those who serve him. Can you

find Bible verses that talk about Jesus' returning with His saints to defend Jerusalem?

2. Which great biblical battle is represented in this chapter?
3. Read Philippians 2:10–11, and describe which scene in this chapter is used to symbolize this biblical event.

CHAPTER 7

1. What does the Wasteland represent?
2. The Prince begins to rule in Arrethtrae. What does this symbolize biblically?
3. The Prince gives authority to His faithful knights to help Him rule in the kingdom. Can you find any Scripture to support this?

CHAPTER 8

1. Cedric tells us that Cullen's good attitude helped the other Knights of the Prince overcome their feelings of apprehension. Have you ever encouraged someone who was afraid to obey God?
2. Cedric encourages the knights in leadership to gain the trust and respect of the people they rule. Why do you think this is wise?
3. Cedric and William enjoy a close relationship that surpasses even that of brothers. Why do you think this is? What does this represent, and can you think of a Bible verse that talks about such a relationship?

CHAPTER 9

1. In this chapter, Cedric teases Talea about her greater age, and Talea replies that she has lived her whole life where age is irrelevant. What is the significance of her statement?

2. Kendra tells the story about how her brother and younger sister became Followers of the Prince, which caused a great division in their family. Later in her story she says she doesn't know what happened to her siblings. What does this symbolize?

3. Earlier in *Kingdom's Reign,* a terrifying creature called a scynth attacks the crew of Cedric's ship. Now we learn more about this beast. From the book of Revelation, can you find what this creature might represent?

4. Cedric and Cullen apprehend the leader of the vicious warriors that attacked the procession of knights. Cedric is initially angry with the man because of his words against the kind of freedom the Prince offers. However, Cedric later pities the man because of his ignorance. One of the great paradoxes of Christianity is that you are most free when you surrender your life to Christ. Have you ever completely surrendered to Christ?

CHAPTER 10

1. In the beginning of this chapter, we read that there are occasional skirmishes with Histen loyalists. What does this symbolize, and why is this significant?

CHAPTER 11

1. Cedric journeys to Chessington to see the Prince. During their visit, the Prince asks Cedric how he is faring in his performance as a knight. When Cedric says he has continued his training, the Prince responds, "Knighthood is in the heart and in the mind." What does this mean?

2. What do you think is significant about the bitter wine?

CHAPTER 12

1. In this chapter, Cedric and Talea duel. What does this symbolize?
2. Cedric realizes that the King gave Arrethtraens the right to choose evil or good. Why do you think the King allowed His people to choose for themselves? What does this represent, and what does it mean for us?

CHAPTER 13

1. In this chapter we finally learn what the secret meetings were all about. What major biblical event is allegorized in this chapter?
2. Why does Jaret choose Alexander Histen over the Prince?

CHAPTER 14

1. Cedric states that "the wicked heart of man" aided in the release of the King's enemies from the Wasteland. Find some Bible verses that talk about the nature of humankind without Jesus.

CHAPTER 15

1. What is the importance of Cedric and Talea's encounter with the scynths?

CHAPTER 16

1. Find the verses in Revelation that are symbolized by Lucius and his evil army surrounding Chessington.

2. What is the significance of the Vactors of Fire? Why does the King use them to execute His judgment on Arreth-trae? What does this symbolize?

CHAPTER 17

1. What does New Chessington symbolize?
2. The Kingdom Series is exciting because it is an allegory of the greatest story ever told. However, what is even more exciting is that this story isn't *just* a story. Everything in the Bible is true. Therefore, not only can you enjoy the drama of this fictional story, you can also be a true follower of Jesus Christ in reality. So I ask just as Cedric did: do you believe?

ANSWERS TO DISCUSSION QUESTIONS

CHAPTER 1

1. The United States of America.
2. The United States and Great Britain played key roles in reestablishing Israel as a nation after World War II, a significant fulfillment of biblical prophecy. Since then, these nations have supported and helped protect God's chosen people through much adversity.

CHAPTER 2

1. In Revelation 5:1–7, God holds a book that is sealed, and an angel asks, "Who is worthy to open the scroll and to loose its seals?" No man was found worthy in heaven or on earth except for Jesus.
2. John 14:6: "I am the way, the truth, and the life. No one comes to the Father except through Me."

CHAPTER 3

1. John 14:2–3.
2. Luke 14:16–24. In this parable the master of the house invites everyone to come, but only a few do.
3. The Life Spice represents God's power over all life in the universe—from the power to heal here on earth to the redemption of our bodies by the Resurrection, as stated in Romans 8:23.

CHAPTER 4

1. Talea represents the children who died in the womb.

CHAPTER 5

1. First Peter 5:8 tells us, "Be sober, be vigilant; because your adversary the devil walks about like a roaring lion, seeking whom he may devour." Lions sneak up on their prey and pounce on them when they least expect it. Therefore, we should never become lackadaisical in our walk of faith.
2. The rise to power of the Antichrist as described in Revelation.
3. Many Bible verses foretell how the Jews will return to the Lord in the last days and finally accept Jesus as their Lord and Savior.

CHAPTER 6

1. Revelation 19:11–16 and Zechariah 14. There are many others.
2. The battle of Armageddon.
3. After the duel between the Prince and Lucius, everyone kneels before the Prince, even His enemies, just as everyone will kneel before Jesus and proclaim Him Lord.

CHAPTER 7

1. The bottomless pit that Satan and his demons are cast into for one thousand years, as described in Revelation 20:1–3.
2. The reign of Jesus Christ as our earthly king.
3. Luke 19:12–19 and Revelation 20:6.

CHAPTER 8

1. Answer based on personal experience.
2. After suffering under Lucius's tyrannical and diabolical

rule, the people of Arrethtrae are probably still leery of anyone in authority. Cullen's direction is also wise because people respond positively to a trustworthy leader.

3. Cedric and William have been given a purpose beyond any other: to serve the Prince. This purpose bonded them through times of persecution and triumph. This represents the fact that when we accept Christ and His calling, we become part of the family of God, which transcends blood ties. A good verse describing such a close friendship is Proverbs 18:24.

CHAPTER 9

1. Just as there is no age in the Kingdom Across the Sea, there is no time in heaven. James 4:14 says, "Whereas you do not know what will happen tomorrow. For what is your life? It is even a vapor that appears for a little time and then vanishes away."

2. Jesus says in Matthew 10:35 and in Luke 12:53 that His truth will divide families, because some will believe and some will not. Kendra didn't know what happened to her siblings because they were taken when the Prince came for them. Read Matthew 24:40–41.

3. In Revelation 9:1–12, a frightful creature rises out of the bottomless pit that is described as being able to torment men like a scorpion. This is one of the seven trumpet judgments and is probably symbolic rather than an actual creature.

4. Answer based on personal experience.

CHAPTER 10

1. The Bible indicates that during the thousand-year reign there will still be sinners. So even though Jesus comes to earth to rule, there will be a need for correction and discipline. The world still isn't paradise because of man's sinful nature and free will to choose right or wrong.

CHAPTER 11

1. This signifies the fact that although we should honor God by following His commandments, it is our hearts and minds that He is most concerned about, for out of the heart flows the important things of life. Read Proverbs 4:23. Also in Revelation 2:23, God says He searches both the hearts and the minds of people.

2. The Bible often mentions sealing the believers of Jesus Christ by the Holy Spirit, as in Ephesians 1:13. Many of the Jews will be sealed to God during the Great Tribulation as well. The bitter wine represents sealing the believers of Jesus and preserving them against the final Day of Judgment.

CHAPTER 12

1. Proverbs 27:17 says, "As iron sharpens iron, so a man sharpens the countenance of his friend." This means it is good to practice your knowledge and skill with another fellow believer, because you both believe in truth.

2. The King didn't want pawns who were forced to obey Him; He wanted people who willingly followed His plans. This represents the free will allowed us by God to

choose between good and evil, and it means that we are free to choose God and His plans or to choose our own way, which ultimately brings pain and sorrow.

CHAPTER 13

1. The release of Satan and his demons from the bottomless pit and the ensuing rebellion that begins. See Revelation 20:7–8.

2. Jaret is enticed by Histen's promise of power. What Jaret foolishly doesn't realize is that Lucius is the father of lies and cannot be trusted. John 8:44 says, "He was a murderer from the beginning, and does not stand in the truth, because there is no truth in him. When he speaks a lie, he speaks from his own resources, for he is a liar and the father of it."

CHAPTER 14

1. Jeremiah 17:9 says, "The heart is deceitful above all things, and desperately wicked; who can know it?" See also Genesis 6:5; 8:21.

CHAPTER 15

1. Their presence in Arrethtrae indicates in a terrifying way that the Wasteland has truly been emptied of all its evil.

CHAPTER 16

1. Revelation 20:7–8. This is the final battle leading to the final judgment of Satan and his demons. This battle should not be confused with Armageddon, which occurs before the millennium and is depicted in chapter 6 of this book.

2. In *Kingdom's Dawn,* the King used the Vactor Deluge to execute judgment on Arrethtrae, and He promised to never again use them. This event represents the Flood during the days of Noah and that God promised to never again destroy the earth by water. This event with the Vactors of Fire represents the final judgment on the earth by God in the form of fire. Revelation 20:9 says, "And fire came down from God out of heaven and devoured them."

CHAPTER 17

1. New Chessington symbolizes the new heaven and new earth God will create for His people. Read Revelation 21:1–11, 22 through 22:21.

2. Romans 10:9 says, "If you confess with your mouth the Lord Jesus and believe in your heart that God has raised Him from the dead, you will be saved." Salvation is a free gift offered by God to anyone who accepts Jesus Christ as his or her personal Savior. In the great apocalyptic book of Revelation, Jesus' tender love and compassion for mankind is explicitly expressed in Revelation 3:20: "Behold, I stand at the door and knock. If anyone hears My voice and opens the door, I will come in to him and dine with him, and he with Me."

Reign of the King

Written for Kingdom's Reign

Music by Emily Elizabeth Black
Edited by Brittney Dyanne Black

AUTHOR'S COMMENTARY

Kingdom's Reign brings to conclusion the allegory of the kingdom of Arrethtrae and its people. It is just a story. The characters of the Kingdom Series are imaginary…but we are not, and the kingdom of God is powerfully more exciting and adventure-filled than that of an allegory. If these books point you to discover the truth of God's Word, then the words were not written in vain.

Kingdom's Reign chronicles the journey of the saints from their entrance into heaven to the return of the saints with Christ in glory, through the millennium, and on to the new heaven and new earth spoken of in the book of Revelation.

It can be appreciated that there are a wide variety of doctrinal beliefs about the end times and the sequence of events as they occur. It is not my intention to promote one theological belief over another concerning the end times. *Kingdom's Reign* was written to bring closure to the series as it attempts to depict the journey's end of mankind. Unlike the biblical and modern history of man up to today, the end-times analogy of *Kingdom's Reign* allowed a substantial amount of literary freedom since the events are not concrete, with characters and circumstances from which to derive the story. This is but one vague interpretation of life after the Rapture concerning the saints and the millennial period on earth.

Certain biblical events are quite evident: Christ will come again to rule on the earth, there will be a millennium period of peace on earth, a new heaven and a new earth will be established by God, and He will live with man forever. All of these elements are included in *Kingdom's Reign,* and as in the other Kingdom Series books, the focus of the entire story is on the Redeemer of mankind, Jesus Christ.

It is my hope, as the author of the words penned here, that you will rediscover a zeal to explore the infallible Word of God and find the courage to remain faithful to Jesus. It is entirely within the realm of possibility that the end-times prophecies spoken of throughout the Bible could begin today. The battle for the hearts of men and women may be drawing to a close. Jesus said we should know the signs of the times. The signs of these times are powerful, and we must be diligent in our knowledge of God's Holy Book. We must be prepared by first accepting the fact that we all desperately need a savior, *the* Savior—Jesus!

> *"And behold, I am coming quickly, and My reward is with Me, to give to every one according to his work. I am the Alpha and the Omega, the Beginning and the End, the First and the Last.... Surely I am coming quickly."*
>
> —REVELATION 22:12–13, 20